Consignment Shop
CONFIDENTIAL

Consignment Shop
CONFIDENTIAL

Short Stories from
a Ladies Consignment shop

Peggy Ann

authorHOUSE®

AuthorHouse™
1663 Liberty Drive
Bloomington, IN 47403
www.authorhouse.com
Phone: 1-800-839-8640

Published by AuthorHouse   08/22/2012

ISBN: 978-1-4772-6102-6 (sc)
ISBN: 978-1-4772-6101-9 (e)

Library of Congress Control Number: 2012914854

Contents

MY EXPERIENCES AS A CONSIGNMENT SHOP OWNER

started writing all these wonderful little stories because I realized after a few pages, how all of our lives and experiences are like a tapestry. We are all interacting with each other and our lives are woven together—for good and bad! HA! I think I read that in a book years ago.

In April 2011, Ira and I decided to start a small ladies consignment shop. We planned it out just like we have done every other business we have owned. We had not owned a business in over four years and we needed to get back to work. The recession was killing us financially.

We laid out our plans. We wanted it to be very clean, unique and look upscale without being upscale.

Our shop would have moderate line clothing all the way up to very high end clothing. We decided we would carry less expensive brands that are new, spotless clean, without flaws and would appeal to the lower income ladies.

We had to take into consideration how bad the economy is now and will be in the future. We do not see the economy coming back in the next 5-10 years. We were ready to put our plans in operation mode.

SHE SCREAMED LIKE A BANSHEE

We filed with the state. We selected the name 'Peggy Ann's Chic Boutique" with the words 'LADIES CONSIGNMENTS' placed right below the name of the shop. After approval with the state, we set out to find a perfect spot. Famous last words. We selected a small inexpensive place in Gulf Gate Village, in Sarasota, Florida. We started looking for fixtures and software for the shop. Much to our surprise a small consignment shop was closing and selling everything right out of the store. Her explanation for her business failure was she was at the end of the street and people turned left at the light before they got to her place. I could smell cigarette smoke on her clothes. I asked, "If she smoked in the shop?" Her response was, "Oh no, never. I always step outside". What a crock!

My husband paid her for the fixtures and asked where all the clothes were that she had consigned. She told him they were all boxed and out front in her van. One of my husband's very few flaws, is he believes most people. She showed him the clothes and I pulled him aside and said no way, she is a smoker and I can smell it in the shop. He kept saying I don't smell a thing. He got her down to next to nothing on over 500 pieces of beautiful clothing. I fretted all the way home. I know when you open those boxes the smell of cigarettes will knock you over. He assured me that would not be the case. She told him they had only been in her van for three days and being boxed the smoke could not get through to the clothes. What a humongous crock. We called someone to come pick everything up and take them to the garage at our home.

She had let the landlord rent the building and the new tenants were moving in on top of her. The new tenant came in and demanded we remove the fixtures that night. It was 9:00 PM and we could not find anyone to move anything for us that late. We promised to have them out by noon the next day. Boy did we get to know the new tenants. It was a lady and her daughter. The lady had bright orange hair and a bald spot on the back of her head. From the get go she kept saying "God Bless you and God is good and God is love". That is why we were frozen in a state of shock when she screamed like a banshee about not having everything out that night. She just kept screaming. When she finally shut up yelling, I told her, "Hey, we are in a mess here too, Missy. We did not know anything about you when we came here to look at the fixtures. Just keep your panties from knotting up and hold strong to your weird way of thinking and we will be out in the morning." She gave out another loud moan and walked away. I started after her and my husband held me back. Her poor little daughter just looked down and tried to act like she did not hear her. They were starting some kind of Latte and WiFi shop. Knew that was doomed right off. National brand coffee shop named Starbucks two blocks away. Panera was just half a block down the street and Gulf Gate Village is littered with little pastry and coffee shops that offer free WiFi.

Their car broke down the next day when we were picking up our fixtures and clothing. We heard them say that they did not have the money to get it fixed. We felt bad, but we remembered how much faith the red headed banshee claimed she had. I bit my tongue to keep from saying, "Don't worry honey, God will heal your car." We just loaded up our goods and left. By the way, her little business venture shut down after three months.

THE ODOR OF R.J. REYNOLDS

I whined all the way home that those boxes are going to knock us over when we open them. My husband said, "Nahhhhh, you watch, they will be fine." I knew he was sweating what they would smell like. He knows I can really get very mouthy and he does not like to give me a reason to whine, "I told you so."

We get home and the movers unload everything and they put the boxes in our laundry room. The time had come to get out the box cutter and see what we had bought. Here we go. He ripped open the first box and lo and behold the room was immediately filled with the aroma of the RJ Reynolds Tobacco Company. It smelled like a bar that had not been aired out for months. I could not bear to jump on him, so I just casually suggested we move all that smelly shit out to the garage or even to the dump where it belonged. I spent all day cleaning the smoke odor off all the fixtures. She was very smart to spray the room before we came to look at fixtures. She also opened all the doors to her van before we looked at the boxes of clothing. Oh well, nothing we can do now but make the best of it. To make a long story short, we spent the next two weeks dry cleaning every piece of the clothing in the dryer with store bought home dryer pads. I went to the store three times and bought a total of 30 boxes of dry cleaning towels. I know the grocery store checker wondered what in the world I was doing with all the cleaning pads. I just kept unloading them onto the checker belt and when I saw the look on her face, I just told her that I was dry cleaning everything I had.

My husband would take the garment off the hanger and stuff it in to the bag and I would start ripping open the little cleaning pads. After a week we had a pretty good system going. We finally got everything cleaned. We dreaded the electric bill since the dryer was going full steam, night and day. I mean night because he felt so guilty about not listening to me about her being a smoker. He would get up in the middle of the night and do a couple of loads. Dear God, we had clothes hanging everywhere, the garage, the laundry room, the garden room, the hallways, the living room and any other place we could store them until we could find a rental space and move everything in. We thought our problem was solved until we started smelling cigarette smoke coming out of everything. Next move we made was cramming everything out into the garage. Fixtures, clothes, and computers, everything was stacked in the garage. We could leave the house and smell the odor when we came back up the driveway. We left the garage open as much as we could and I made trips back to the grocery store to buy febreze in sheets and many, many bottles of febreze spray to eliminate the odor. We used over 20 boxes of the sheets and 10 bottles of the spray. Our routine was, get up in the morning and spray the clothes and fixtures in the garage and put out more febreze sheets. Then before we go to bed spray again and put out the sheets. We did that for over a week. This was done while negotiating a lease for a space to house our little shop. We were on a roll, the odor was almost gone and the clothes were beautiful. Then as luck would have it, he got in a rush one evening and grabbed the spray bottle before going to bed and sprayed into the air what he thought was the febreze. I walked out and smelled bleach and started yelling Oh My Gauze!!! What are you doing?" He turned around and said, "Spraying just like we always do." I yelled, "OMG, look at the bottle you are spraying tub cleaner with bleach in it". Luckily most of the clothes were covered with plastic bags we had bought to use later. Let's see, he spot bleached two Ralph Lauren cashmere jackets, five sweaters from Christian Dior, a Channel suit and several designer dresses. One was Vintage Lilly. I yelled as I yanked the things off the hangers and threw them in the trash, "you have really done it now". He looked so sad and so hurt, I put my arm around him and said, "Oh well it could have been a lot worse. At least you missed the Cache. Didn't you?" "The what?" He asked. "The beautiful green Cache, you know the two piece outfit with the beautiful tie waist", as I raised up the sheet and looked at the brand new tye/dye outfit. The bleach had hit the front of it and it was running down the middle like a rainbow. Forget it I said, "We will just deduct that from your first paycheck". I felt sorry for him because he looked mortified at what he had done.

TATTOO PARLOUR

We got up the next morning and the movers came and took all the items over to the little space we had rented. No sooner had we paid the movers and started to install the wall mounted garment racks, then in walked our landlord with an announcement. "I just rented the unit right next door to you to a Tattoo Parlor". She appeared to be proud that she had done this. I stood there in shock and then I looked at her and said, "Please tell me this is a joke and you are kidding." "No", she said "They will be moving in two weeks." My reply to her, "You just doomed our business. You just sank us before we even got off the ground." She was surprised we were upset about a tattoo guy moving in right beside us. She said, "Oh don't worry his hours are going to be from 4:00 in the afternoon to midnight or later". I yelled, "Do you realize what my little old lady customers will do when they see Tattoo Parlor printed on his sign right next to mine? You have got to be nuts to do this to anyone, especially a new business just starting out." She had a great comeback which I know she did not expect me to take her up on her offer. She snapped, "Well, if you don't like it, I will refund all your money and let you out of your lease and you can move out".

Remember I had just paid utilities, movers, painters and carpenters. No sooner had she made her offer than I yelled, "That's a deal. We will be out in a couple of days". My poor husband is standing there like where are we going to go, there are no other places available except the one around the corner in the newly renovated building and it is double the rent here. She stormed out and yelled, "You can pick up your check when you move out and give me the keys back". We knew she never thought that would happen. I raced around the corner and got the phone number of the only place in the area to lease. I called and the landlord said someone backed out of a lease that very morning. I asked how much and haggled with him and he came over and we signed the lease right then. We called the same movers and they were elated to make the money all over again.

They came two days later and we moved again. Oh yes, the landlord that leased to a tattoo parlor owned six units all lined up on that one street. She now has four of them empty. I remember my last and final words to her. Leasing to a tattoo guy was not a very business-like move, especially when you had a travel agency, an upscale teenage clothing shop and a baby specialty store right there in your spaces. Not a smart move at all. Really, really dumb move. She just laughed at me. Poetic Justice. Well that cost us an extra $700 to move and transfer all the utilities, not to mention all the renovations we did to her lousy building. Lot of good it did her, most of the units are sitting there empty now.

SECOND START, SECOND LOCATION

We started planning to put all of our fixtures and goods in place. Counters had arrived, utilities were on again, we had hired three ladies to help get the place set up for business. One was a neighbor with a very southern drawl, the other was the young banker that helped us set up our banking accounts and the last was a lady that had lived in the area all her life and she was needing to work for free or as she put it, "do volunteer work so she could qualify for a grant to go to school to be a pharmacist." This was the first part of April and she needed 90 hours before August 15, 2011.

We all got to work and the next two weeks were very productive. We set all the fixtures in place and got the dressing rooms all set up and hung all the clothes on the racks. The store had the full blown scent of Mountain Mist febreze. It was just heavenly. Trust me it was the only thing that had the odor of anything heavenly. I heard this little tapping on the front glass door and when I opened the door, this snotty middle aged brunette came waltzing into the store. She said "I work for your competition and I just wanted to take a look around". I tried to be nice and I did my best to block her path by running my mouth, "I came from Texas ten years ago love it here, don't you?" She just ignored me and stuck up her nose and snorted, "Oh, we don't carry this brand, they are cheap and we can't mark them up as much." My husband looked at me with his brows raised and I could tell he was saying in code, "Please don't knock her down and kill her right here, we have a big grand opening planned and we cannot afford bail for you."

He stepped up and said, "We are planning a big Grand Opening; please tell your owner you all are welcome to attend." She just kept her nose in the air and floated out. Not a thank you or kiss my behind or anything. Oh by the way, she had the gall to ask how much we were paying our employees. I said, "we pay $15-20 and hour. Her mouth dropped and she said maybe I will have to work for you. After she left, the ladies all looked at each other and said, "Hey, I am not getting that kind of pay are you?"

THE GRAND OPENING

We had planned the big grand opening for April 15, but had to delay to April 30 since we had to move twice and set-up the second building. The big day was here and we were expecting around 30-35 people. We had closer to 70 people. They came from all over. We had run several ads and mailed out fliers to all kinds of business women. Some of them drove 40 miles to get here. What a great surprise!

So many of the local people told us how glad they were that we had opened our little shop. The Grand Opening was a huge success. Refreshments were donated by the local French Bakery. Many of the local business owners stopped by to welcome us to the area. We were off to a great start. Nothing can stop us now, so we hoped!

The Grand Opening was not totally flawless. A lady came in and brought things to be consigned.

She had gone to the other consignment shop first. The manager looked at her clothes and said, "Oh, we don't take things like this. Just take them down to Peggy Ann's, she takes all kinds of junk." Ira was standing there and whispered in my ear, "Let go, just let it go. Just consider it a good referral". He was clinching my arm so I would not throw a fit. The clothes were beautiful and I accepted all of them. She was one of my first consignors.

MORE INFORMATION THAN NEEDED

The business is going great now, but the employees we hired for part time shifts are not working out as we expected. The young banker that worked for us on Saturdays was the first to bite the dust. We were dumbstruck when in the middle of the day and a shop full of customers she announced to my husband the amount of money we had taken into the account that stores our credit card charges. She proceeds to tell him in front of customers how much we made each day the week before. He never said a word to her. He waited until Monday morning and called the bank branch manager and asked her to block our account. The manager said she could not do that and wanted to know why. When he told her one of their employees was snooping into our account she said, "I am sorry but I have no control over that."

My husband's response was, "Well, I have control over it, I will just change banks after being with you for over 10 years". He did just that. Not without expense though. New checks and the whole enchilada. We told the young lady we would call her when we needed her again. Well, that is not going to happen. One down two more to go.

THEN ANOTHER ONE BITES THE DUST

emember the lady that came to us with the story about needing 90 volunteer hours, totally not true. She started out really working hard and helping us and when we needed heavy things done or wall racks hung. She called her boyfriend and he worked several days for us without pay. They insisted that they loved people and just wanted to help us. We were suspicious, but we had nothing to steal at this point. Two weeks into them playing the innocent little, "all we want to do is help you all get the store open", she got sick and couldn't come in at all for four days. She said she has MS. That made us feel really sorry for her. Then she came back looking like she had been on a weeklong binge of some kind. She came in bearing gifts from the local Goodwill store. Very nice hat boxes and flower arrangements. We put them around the store as it was almost finished and getting close to April 30, our Grand Opening Day. The next day she did not show up again and was out sick the next three days.

When she finally came back to work, she looked even worse. Dirty clothes and very puffy and hung over looking. She was in a horrible mood and gripped about everything. She took the caulk gun and covered every corner in the dressing room. It was a mess. I sent her home and later that evening called and told her not to come back, because this was not working out. We thought that was the end of it. Not hardly. The next day her boyfriend showed up and demanded back pay for both of them. He also wanted to be paid for the items she had brought in from Goodwill. He started yelling at me when I told him that we did not ask her to buy the things and he was welcome to pick them up and take them to her. He started screaming and it was really bad timing. We had three customers in the place, and two of them, very elderly ladies, took out running out the front door. There was a lady there from Michigan that was looking at shoes and she dialed 911. She was very brave and was not going to leave us. We have a silent security alarm. My husband ran over and kept pushing the button. What a way to find out that it was not connected properly and did not work when he pushed it. He started yelling that he had pushed the panic alarm and the guy turned and took out running. He got into his truck and peeled rubber. The two elderly ladies came back in and they had called the police too. The police arrived and he was gone. We told them the entire story about how they needed the hours of volunteer work to qualify for a grant to go to pharmaceutical school. They looked up the address and their names and they needed a pharmaceutical grant alright.

They were both on probation for drug abuse. Man did we feel stupid. Again we accept people for what they say until they prove their story is different. We feel very fortunate that they did not hurt anyone. The alarm company came and fixed the silent alarm and the police probably read those two people the riot act. We have not seen them since. We should have been a little suspicious when she told us the story about being kidnapped and held hostage for 10 hours by a man that had done this to 15 other women. She told us that she had been on TV News with some of the other women that were victims of this very violent man. She said that there was a swat team of 150 FBI agents and policemen that rescued her. What a tall tale. Both of us are just glad to be rid of them. The police told them to stay away from us or they would go back to jail. Man, we felt like the biggest suckers in the world. Oh well, the second one down.

SOUTHERN BELLE

*L*ast but not least comes the story about the little middle aged Southern Bell. What a slow drawl she has.

She worked really hard right up to the Grand Opening, and then it all went downhill. She could not give change, she could not arrange shoes by their sizes on the shelf without one of us walking her through it.

It was really nuts. I was waiting on a customer and listening to how she could not give change for a sale that was $9.88, when the customer gave her a ten dollar bill. She just kept counting and talking and saying, "Just wait a minute, just wait a minute, I will get there". The lady finally said, "Just keep the twelve cents" and walked out. After this happened several times, we told her we would call her when we needed help. The customers loved her, we loved her. The UPS driver loved her. The Postman loved her.

The FED-X driver would stare at her and hang around to hear her talk. But dammit, she could not make change! We hated to see her go. She comes in to visit the shop often. She is a 5' tall "Suzanne Sugarbaker," on steroids. You either love her or hate her! Not much in between.

We have decided that we will run the little business by ourselves. Just the two of us until we either get too tired or it gets too big for us to take care of it. No more part time help.

WHO AM I AND WHAT AM I DOING HERE?

The month of May was very interesting. We picked up many more consignor's and customers than we ever imagined we would. One of our first consignors was a little, old, orange headed, 4' tall lady that dyed her own hair. She was very frail and very senile. It took her almost three hours to get from her house to our shop, which was about a mile. She kept calling and saying "Where are you, have you moved? Tell me how to get to your place". I would tell her and then when she finally made it within a block of us; she called again and said "I don't see you. Where are you?" I asked where she was and she was on the next street over, so I walked to the corner and kept talking to her to go to the stop sign and turn left and that she would see me standing there waving at her. She drove right past me and rounded the corner again. Twice she passed me and twice I was jumping up and down waving to her. Finally, I ran out in the street and she saw me. She drove very, very slowly while I directed her to turn in our drive way and park in front of the shop. Finally she had arrived.

I walked over and opened the car door and she said, "Where have you been, I have been looking for you". I helped her out and she used her cane to get into the front door. We have a single story building and she asked where the stairs were so she could visit the artist upstairs. We told her there was no upstairs. She just kept insisting he was upstairs. The only way to shut her up was to tell her that he had moved last week and we did not know where he went. She consigned her clothing and then turned around and decided to buy a blouse and pants that she had just consigned. There was no convincing her that she could take them free of charge because they were hers. We finally charged her and put the things in a bag and she was happy.

She lost her keys in the store somewhere so we had a major hunting party going on. We found her keys and she left the store and got in the car and I noticed her cane was there by the counter. I grabbed the walking cane and raced out the front door and stopped her. She rolled the window down and I told her she had forgotten her cane and tried to hand it to her. She said she did not have a walking cane and hold on to it because someone would come back for it. I tried to tell her she came in with it and there was no reasoning with her. I finally got desperate and told her that it was my cane and I really wanted her to have it as a gift. She was so moved she nearly cried. She thanked me several times and drove off into the sunset or towards the beach, which scared the hell fire out of both of us. Nothing we could do, so we just said a quiet prayer that she would not drive off the Siesta Key Bridge. Kind of had the feeling she should not be driving anymore.

HE WAS MY BEST FRIEND

One afternoon in May, we had a dark haired lady about mid 50's came in and she was just looking around and I greeted her. She asked where I was from, I told her Texas. Most people notice my Texas accent the minute I open my mouth. We started talking and she started telling me a story about how last week her boyfriend drowned. She was sobbing and telling us that the lifeguards did not go after him and she is not a good swimmer. When they would not help him, she went in and pulled him on to the beach. They left him on his back and did not do CPR. She blamed them completely because he died. She was sobbing and saying, "If they had only been trained and turned him over on his side or stomach, maybe he would have made it. He was my best friend", she kept saying between sobs. Then she caught me off guard. She said, "I really don't want to live, I have thought seriously about killing myself so I could be with him." I was stunned. I told her that was not an answer and it would just take time to get over her grieving. She calmed down and tried on some dresses and decided on a blouse. She paid for it and started to leave. I kept saying please stay in touch with us so we know how you are doing. I will always be sorry for not hugging her before she left.

SPRINKLE IT WITH HOLY WATER

$\mathcal{T}$he business is really taking off and we are very pleased with the way it is starting to pay off. I got a call one morning from a lady with a heavy Hispanic accent. She asks what kind of clothes I was accepting. I told her spotless clean, on hangers, and they did not have to be name brand items. She said she would bring things in the following week. I had almost forgotten about her phone call when she came in our front door.

She drove up in a worn out old jeep and started bringing things into the store. I thought oh boy these things are going to be awful. She dragged in a huge old box and started taking things out of it. Shoes that were still in the boxes, brand new designer shoes. Then the handbags still wrapped in tissue paper and in shopping bags. Then, the dresses that were on hangers and had the tags still on them. They were all designer and top of the line items. We asked her where in the world she got all the wonderful merchandise. Her story started to unfold.

She was a top of the line well known image consultant and she dressed very rich ladies from coast to coast. She had studied fashion in Italy and France and been working the last few years out of Palm Beach. Then the bomb shell. Her rich lady clients were not able to use her services anymore because the economy had gone south and their husbands had lost their money. Her business finally dried up and she lost her beautiful home on eight acres by the river. She lives in the very, very rich part of Florida where the homes have airplane hangars. Her home was in foreclosure and her husband left her for another woman when the going got rough. She said "I drove a Mercedes and a Jag and now I drive a POS". I ask her, "What in the world is a POS'. Her reply was, "a Piece of Shit". "It is the old car we used to drive our four German shepherds to the vet and take them for a ride".

"Now it is all I have to drive. My husband took both our cars and left me with this POS. Every time I need to drive it, I feel like I have to pray over it and sprinkle it with holy water, just to get me where I need to go. So far so good. I have no money if it breaks down. I am selling everything I have to feed my dogs and myself. They are my babies. He took everything I had. He cleaned out my bank accounts. I have an invention and had saved my money to market it and he took all that money. I have nothing to live on. Just get whatever you can for my things. I need the money". We sold a lot of her things and she made three trips back to our stop with her clothing. Everything she brought in was new and still had the tags attached.

One afternoon last week she came in the front door. It was one of the times she was not crying. She had been so depressed about everything and now she was mad. In fact she was furious. She had a car load of her husband's clothes that he was coming to pick up later. I walked out to her car and she said, "I think I will just dump them in the middle of the parking lot here and run over them". She started to take them out of the back end of the old broken down jeep and I stopped her. I said, "Sweetie let's not do that. There is a big dumpster around the back of my building.

Just pull your car around and I will go through and meet you back there". She said, "That sounds like a good plan". She pulled out of the parking lot and headed to the dumpster in back and I ran through the building to meet her back there. My husband asked me where I was going and I said, "I will tell you later".

When she got back there we pulled everything out of her car that belonged to him and we threw it over into the dumpster. She did not shed another tear after that. In fact as she drove off she yelled, "Boy, do I feel much better. I just unloaded a lot of trash". I guess that is what she said. Her accent is so heavy, she might have said "good riddance, you ugly POS of a husband". Then, I went back into the building through the back door, my husband asked me where in the world I had been. I said, "Oh just out back with our Latino friend dumping some trash out of her car." He asked, "Is she OK?" I told him, "Yep, she feels pretty good today."

She has been back in several times with various items. I have not seen her depressed anymore. Just mad as hell at being treated so badly and determined to make things work without his help. Bet we see her on Home Shopping Network in the next couple of years. I would bet she becomes very rich and famous.

GOSSIP AND PINK BAGS

We are growing our business more and more every day. Ladies come through the front door and tell us that they like our store much more than the consignment store in this area. My husband told me not to comment when they tell us how rude the other store owner is to them. I promised him I would quit agreeing with them and just say, "I am so sorry, but we will not be rude to you. We appreciate your business." He warned me that the universe would teach me a lesson if I did not stop telling the customers that I know what you mean, they are just awful. I promised him that I would not say another word.

One day I broke my promise and let loose with my own humble opinion about my competitor. We did not make a sale for the next two days. He said, "See that is what happens when you gossip. You get punished". I swear that has happened to me twice. I will try very hard not to say anything negative about the competition again. Right now I have my own little contest going. The competitor uses pink bags. I want to see nothing but red bags going down the sidewalk, I have a goal to wipe out the pink bags. He warns me not to get too caught up in the color of the bags or the universe will come after me again. I can't help myself. I don't want those pink bags out on the sidewalk because everyone in the area knows what color bags each shop uses.

SMELLY CAT, SMELLY CAT

Next is a story about a very wealthy woman that brought in 74 items to consign with us. Everything was beautiful on the first glance. Then she left and we started going through the clothes and finding something sprayed all over them. There were yellow stain and everything had blonde and white hair on it. About half way through checking her things in, we started wheezing, our eyes itched and our noses started running. We could not figure what the heck was going on. Then we realized what the stains and the hair on the clothes were. It was cat pee and cat hair. We yelled when we realized what it was, "OMG these things are covered with cat pee and cat hair. Cover them up. No, put them all back in the boxes. Call the lady and ask if she has a cat". I got her on the phone and started telling her what was happening to us. I finally asked her if she has a cat. Her reply, "Oh not just one cat, I have five cats." I said, "My husband has asthma and I cannot accept your clothes they have cat urine sprayed all over them". "Oh my goodness," she said, "I knew they got all over the clothes and sometimes peed on them but I did not think it was all over everything I brought you". I tried to keep my cool and asked her what she wanted me to do with her things.

I wanted to burn them, but her decision was to donate them to charity and get her a receipt. It was around $2,000 worth of used designer clothing. A good Coach bag with cat spray all over it. A perfect

Dana Buchman sweater set with cat urine sprayed all over it. The dresses from Niemen's and Italy with cat hair and urine all over them. It broke my heart. I get 50% of all the things I sell in our shop. What a loss. I guess she loved her cats too much to keep them out of her closet. I drove them to the local charity and explained what I had for a donation. I told them a lot of them had cat hair and urine on them and they took them and said they would sort through everything. I probably won't ever go back to their store again. I would be afraid the things I gave them would cause me to sneeze and wheeze.

CAT OWNERS BEWARE

We now have a very large sign and firm policy. "*WE DO NOT ACCEPT ITEMS FROM ANYONE THAT OWNS A CAT. SOME OF OUR EMPLOYEES HAVE ASTHMA AND IT IS TO RISKY TO PUT CAT CONTAMINATED ITEMS IN OUR STORE.*" We have had a couple of instances where customers brought things in anyway. When I looked at the clothes I said, very nicely, "Please take your clothes back to your car. My husband has asthma attacks and your cat contaminated clothes could cause him to get seriously ill". If they hesitate or protest, my husband knows the routine. He starts coughing and sneezing and grabbing his throat. Boy, do they grab their things and run out. He puts on a pretty good show for them.

THE BROWN BAG SPECIAL

We love the people that come in and ask if we are accepting consignments. I say, "Yes, if they are spotless clean and on hangers. They do not have to be designer clothes". They say, "I will get them out of the car and bring them in". Here they come in a few minutes carrying a greasy brown bag and plop it down on the front counter. I stand on my toes and peek in and see clothes all wadded up and filthy and say, "There is no way I can take these. They are wrinkled and dirty". One lady snapped back, "Well don't you do laundry here? Don't you clean all the clothes up before putting them on the racks?" I said, "No we don't. I barely get my husband's clothes washed". She yanked up the greasy brown bag and stomped out. Man do I want to tell some of these people off. I don't because it would not be good for our business. We have some total nitwits bringing Shitttttt in to try and make some money.

We have one lady that goes to garage sales and picks up clothing and runs in and leaves them on the counter when we are busy. Last time she tried that. I took the clothes and threw them back at her and said, "Please stop bringing me clothes from your garage sale shopping. I appreciate your trying to make a living this way, but not at our expense. Please, we do not have time to call you to come back and pick up your rejects". I wanted to say, don't come back in unless you are buying. We do not want your junk. I bit my tongue though. One time she came in and wiped her nose on a dress and handed it to me. I gave it back as she was telling me that she had the flu and was going home to get in bed. I stepped back and said, "Why in the world are you coming around us when you are sick?" "Oh, I won't get too close," she whined, as she sneezed. A few days later I got a horrible cold and was sick for a week. Guess I am not much better because I had to work all week with her cold. Not sure which one of us is the most thoughtless. Her coming in when she was so sick or me working around my customers with a cold. What do you do when you have no employees and you have to keep the store open?

BANKER'S WIFE

We picked up a consignor that is a Banker's wife. She is a real piece of work. She can name every clothing designer that is known to mankind and then some. She loves to drop names that she knows we have no idea who she is talking about. We both get a knot in the pit of our stomach every time she comes in the front door, which is about three times a week. It is incredible the time she spends chasing down every little thing her daughter wants to take back to college. It is really sad for both of them. Every waking minute is spent shopping for just the perfect name brand outfit. We try and overlook things she says. She has no idea how insulting she really is. She is like a "wanna be name dropper of clothing brands". She wants to bring her things in and get top dollar, but she doesn't want to pay anything for them when she buys from us.

It is very hard not to get very angry with her. She gives off the vibes of being more knowledgeable and better educated than we are. I don't really think it is her intent, but she is doing a good job of trying to be uppity. She continually goes on about how much better the designers in Europe are than the designers here in the USA. We both wonder how in the world she has time to do anything else, because she spends 24 hours a day shopping. She even brags that her daughter ordered some of her clothing from China so she could get exactly what she wanted. Man she is just totally obsessed with buying things and shopping all day every day. It is like an addiction. She makes us cringe to see her coming and relieved to see her going out the front door. She comes in and interrupts my husband when he is trying to do computer work and wants him to drop everything and look up her account and see if anything has sold. Aggravating. Just one of the things that goes along with being a business owner. Her college daughter is so snotty that she is too good to even come into our store. She just waits in the car or stands outside. We both wonder if she is embarrassed to be in a consignment shop.

THE NICER CONSIGNER

Not all our customers are nuts. We have a lady named Sherry that comes into our store about once a week. She is like a shining light. When she comes in the front door it makes everything better for both of us. She is smiling and laughing and always telling us how nice the store looks. If anyone should be mean and disagreeable, it should be her. She has been married twice to totally abusive husbands. She is twice divorced and has been raising a Downs Syndrome child for 45 years. She brings in nice items from time to time and always has a funny story to tell us about her condo association. She has only one real flaw. She believes everything she hears on FOX news. She loves Shawn Hannity and Rush Limbaugh. I have allowed her to live with this opinion because she is so nice otherwise. Sometimes when she gets wound up, I clear the air for a few minutes by saying, "FOX news is nothing more than a Dallas Series Soap Opera". She snaps back to reality and we start talking about things like the weather. We love to see her coming. Wish more of our customers were like her.

LADY FROM BOSTON

$\mathcal{L}$ ate one afternoon, a lady came into the shop. She was a nut case! She would pick up a necklace and say, "I want to see how this necklace looks on you, put it on!" She would step back and stare. Then she decided I needed to wrap a scarf around my neck, so she could see how they looked together. I did my best to follow her orders, considering I am not good at following anyone's orders.

After thirty minutes of her having me model necklaces and scarves, she had the nerve to tell me to hold different colors and sizes of purses, so she could see how they looked. She wanted to see if she liked a shoulder bag or a regular handbag. By this time, I was getting fed-up. Enough already! I told her there were other customers I needed to help. She snapped, "I'm from Boston, I am used to being waited on". OMG, I can't believe she just said that to me, "Peggy Ann". I tossed the purses back on the shelf and yanked the scarf and necklace off and threw them on the counter. I stood straight up, all 5'2" of me, looked her in the eye and said, "I am from Texas and I don't cater to rude people". She looked shocked and turned on her heels and left the shop.

I looked at Ira and threw my head back and said, "That was not a good idea for her to come in here and try to give me orders. You and I both know, I am not some little ole Texas piss-ant she could push around.

Especially, since this happened on the same day that the 20 year old window washer told you, he wanted to see the "Older Lady", she hired me to wash the windows. That remark was still stuck in my craw when the lady from Boston came in and started issuing her orders".

THE WATCH VS THE THREE BEARS

esterday we had a lady come in who was newly retired. She was shopping for a watch. I had just taken in around a dozen very nice watches with brand new batteries. They were very upscale and very beautiful watches. We also had the new Jelly watches that are like rubber, like the old swatch watches. We had them in eight different colors. I started showing her watches and this is how it went. First the white jelly watches because she wanted a white band. "Oh no, that is not the right color of white". OK how about the black one. "Oh no, that reminds me of death". Okay let's look at the gold one. "Oh no, that is to dull, I need color". OK let's move on and look at the real watches. Maybe a nice Geneva in a silver tone. "Oh no, that is too nice". How about a brown band with a large face. "No, that makes me feel old. I can still see". This went on for about 15 minutes and then she went back to the large jelly watches. I showed her the pink one and she slapped it on her wrist and declared it would make her arm too hot and made her sweat. I looked at her and said, "Well dear God, this is like the three bears. Isn't it? This one is too hot, this one is too cold, and AWWWW this one is just right.

"We just can't find one that is just right, so I will just let you look around, I have no more watches in the shop to show you." Her response, "Oh that is OK, I really didn't want a watch today anyway." My husband looked at me like, "Please don't pop her one. She is bigger than both of us". She tried on about 60 pairs of shoes and left. Thank you God for my husband reminding me that some people would really try my nerves.

This reminded me of the day a mother and daughter came in and tried on lots of outfits and when they left, I walked into the dressing room and found a huge pile of clothes in the middle of the floor wrong side out and hangers all mixed in with them. I could not believe what a horrible example that mother is for her daughter. How stupid and rude it is to walk out and feel like it is the maid's job to clean up after you. Most of our customers hang them on the rack outside the dressing room door.

BRITISH LOVE HANDLES

We have a lovely customer with a very distinct British accent. She is probably in her 70's and slightly slumped over with many, many love handles up and down her back and front. In other words, she has a (excuse my description) very dumpy and stocky type figure. She comes in every Tuesday morning and looks at everything. She always finds something. Today she found the blouses with spandex stretch in them. A young lady had brought in four of them the day before. They are for a younger woman with no lumps or bumps on the body. The colors were blue, white, red and yellow. Guess which one she grabbed? Yep, the bright cherry red and she took it into the dressing room like it was a treasure to behold. Hence, she emerged wearing the poor little red blouse with the seams about to burst.

It stretched across her back with the lumps and bulges blossoming out all over. Front and back were truly a sight to behold. My husband decided to move away from the front of his desk. He told me later, he was afraid if she exhaled, the top would explode and he could lose an eye or break the lens in his glasses from a stray button. She had really huffed and puffed and worn herself out just getting all the buttons closed. She declared with a huge smile on her face in her British accent, "This is the most beautiful blouse. It is so fig-gur flattering. It just hugs everything. Don't you agree?" I knew not what to say, I drew in a deep breath and lied like a dog. "Oh my, my, my, that is truly something. Isn't that little blouse cute?"

"My goodness it would look wonderful with this beautiful cream colored jacket". The jacket was hanging by the front register so I helped her get it on. I tried not to make eye contact with my husband, because we both try to be very honest when a customer asks our opinion. This time it would have broken her heart. I did not want her going out in that blouse and telling her friends I helped her pick it out. How grateful I was that she loved the jacket. It was truly my lucky day. She left very prim and British proper with every bump and bulge covered. Thank God for that cream colored jacket.

"PETTICOAT JUNCTION"

$\mathcal{N}$ow we are going into the rainy season. In Florida, the month of June brings lots of afternoon rain storms. The sun was shining brightly and then all of a sudden we got our first rain since we opened the shop. It started raining about noon and kept pouring for the next hour. People were still coming into the shop, rain and all. Even our former employee, the little Southern Belle with the heavy southern drawl. She came running into the shop and started shaking like a wet dog. She said, "Before I start to shop, I need to pee." I said, "Well you know where it is, go for it." She went to the back of the store and no sooner had she entered the ladies room when she screamed, "Wadda, Wadda it is floodin' the whole bathroom". We went running to the back of the building and lo and behold the dam had broken and the flood water was pouring in. She pulled off her shoes and was wadding through two inches of water in the bathroom. She stated that all that wadda just made her want to pee more than when she came in the front door.

The entire back of the building, for about six feet from the wall, was standing in water. We opened the back door and the entire alley was standing in six inches of water. It was coming in everywhere. We were helpless to stop this monsoon. We could only use the four little towels we had to try and stop some of the damage. When all else fails just move everything to the front of the store and go on like nothing was happening.

My husband looked out the back door and saw that the florist next door had built a rain catcher. It consisted of a large barrel with little pink ribbons and petticoat netting tied around it to make it look pretty. It really looked like something out of Petticoat Junction. The rain was pouring off the roof down the rain spout and into her crappy gigantic barrel. It was not pointed her way, but was aimed right at our wall and back door. It was like a huge fire hose aimed right at our back door. When all the shouting and sloshing was over, we called the landlord and told him we needed an Ark. His daughter came out and said it was the rain barrel that had caused all the problems. She went next door to the Florist and the next thing we knew the "shit had hit the fan". The landlord told her that the barrel needed to come down because it was flooding the unit next door. The landlord left and the next thing we knew hammers were banging and boards were flying. She had called her husband to come take the barrel down right now. She was furious. How dare we be upset because her stupid barrel had flooded our shop. She thought that piece of crap was cute back there in the alley where wino's come around at night after we close. They pee'd on the legs of the cutesy little barrel and left their beer cans all around it. For all we knew they probably took a bath in it. The rain barrel was gone, but the Hatfield and McCoy feud had just begun. All this over the damn "Petticoat Junction" rain barrel.

SIGN BE GONE

We bought a portable sign to put out by the street each morning. The third night we left for the day we forgot to bring our sign in. The next morning it was gone! Gone like a freight train! Gone like the wind! Just gone! We paid over $200 for the sign and the stand that held it. We walked around and started asking if anyone else lost their sign. The jeweler, with the bad military haircut said, "Yeah, mine got picked up last night too. All you have to do is call Code Enforcement. Jim probably has your sign in his building. Call him and ask if he picked it up last night." Call, we did, and yes, he had our sign and he would bring it back to us in about an hour. You get three free times and then he will write you a ticket. We now have a note by the front door reminding us to bring in the sign. So far, so good. We haven't forgotten it again. He not only brought our sign back but he brought back five signs that he had pulled up that belonged to the jeweler. Never left our sign out overnight again. Quick note! The jeweler, is very good friends with the florist. He took her side in the "Rain Barrel" feud. We got the cold shoulder for several months. No big loss.

OLD LADY FARTS

*B*ack to the customers that come into our shop. Last week we had a lady and her 90 year-old mother come in. The 90 year-old mother picked out a few things to try on and her daughter took them into the dressing room for her. The daughter left her to try on the clothes while she looked around. The store was starting to get busy and everyone was looking around and the music is playing Frank Sinatra "Fly Me to the Moon" in the background. All of a sudden the old lady let the biggest FART known to mankind. Not once but about a dozen times. Everyone looked around and tried to play like they did not hear it. Oh my God, we thought if she doesn't stop right now, she will clear the building. Her daughter did nothing. She acted like she did not even notice. That was not the worst of it. The old lady came walking out of the dressing room in totally nothing but her underpants. No bra, just saggy underpants. My husband took a nose dive under his desk. She asked her daughter to help her find another pair of pants and the daughter, unruffled, very casually walked her over to the pants rack and her mother chose a pair that she liked. She went back into the dressing room and continued to try on clothes and let about 50 fast and furious farts fly. We have never been so glad to see customers leave. They waved when they left and said, "we will see you again next week. We love this little shop". I swear they left and everyone started laughing. It was like, we can't believe we just witnessed that. Maybe next time I will turn the music up louder when I see them coming.

BANISHED FROM THE PENTHOUSE

My next customer story will ruffle the feathers of any woman that believes she can stand on her own two feet and take care of herself. This beautiful older lady, maybe around 60ish, came in to consign with us. She had obviously been lifted, twisted, nipped and tucked quite a few times. She brought her little dog in with her. It was a pretty little Bichon that was getting very old. I think she said twelve years old. The little thing was named Emma and she was almost deaf and blind. She told me not to lean down and pet the little dog because she might bite me. "Oh, OK, she is old and doesn't feel friendly any more". "NO," she said, "My new boyfriend is mean to her because he does not like dogs. We live in a Penthouse in Downtown and he told me the dog is not allowed to live there anymore because it barked at him when he used his foot to kick her out of his path to the bathroom. It is OK though, my mother just died recently and left me a little run down place outside of town. I leave her over there at night and then I pick her up during the day and take her shopping with me." I asked who stayed with her at night. She said, "Oh no one. I just give her dinner and water and leave her there".

I could not believe my ears. I told her that I have two little Yorkies and I would never leave them alone out in a country house or anywhere else without someone being there with them in case of an emergency. Me and my big mouth. I asked her, "Why in the world she would allow him to kick her poor little dog and why she preferred his company over the little dog. Why in the world don't you tell him to get lost? Who needs a man like that?" She was very surprised at how upset I got about her little dog being mistreated. Well her response floored me. She said in a baby talk voice, "I don't own the Penthouse, he does and I like living in the Penthouse. I like this kind of lifestyle. Doggie doesn't mind living in the other little house. She does not know the difference. I do not want to mess up a good thing I have going with my boyfriend." I just looked at her with disgust and said, "You have no clue what a shallow mess you are living in and what a short term you have at that beloved Penthouse. You just have no clue at all". She did not respond at all. I figured that would be the last I would ever see of her. She came in today and consigned fifteen garments that were beautiful. Neither one of us even mentioned our last conversation. Her little dog was not with her.

RIDING THE RAIL TO COLORADO

Today was a good day, a few strange people, but a good day. Early this morning an elderly lady came in looking for a jacket to wear to Colorado. She tried on several jackets and I was more than willing to help until I realized she had a lisping and spitting problem. I kept trying to dodge every time she talked. Certain words made spit fly out of her mouth and down the front of her blouse. She hit me a couple of times, but after about ten minutes, I had learned that if I stepped back when she started to speak, I could avoid the spit missiles. I finally got out of her that she was trying to sell her house and move to Colorado. From the things she was saying and spitting at me, I could tell she had the first nickel her husband ever made for her. She was quibbling over a Ralph Lauren cashmere jacket that still had the tag hanging on it and was probably around $350-$400 originally. We had a price tag of $12 on it and it was in perfect condition. She wanted me to reduce the price. I told her that was a giveaway price and I could not do the consignor that way. Her reply was "Well honey, I just don't know if I need to spend that much money". I snapped back at her my favorite saying, "When in doubt, just do without."

I helped her get the jacket off and started to hang it back up. She said well let me go to the car and see if I can scrape up $12.00, will you drop the tax. By this time I was tired of dodging spit and putting up with her haggling. I told her $12.00 would be fine. The old ding bat went to the car and came back with a $100 bill and still did not want to pay the tax. Her final parting statement was, "Can you believe I have to pay $1,200 to ship my car out to Denver when I move. Isn't that a rip off?" I wanted to say, "Not hardly you old fruitcake. The rip off was me letting you spit your way in here and waste my time for almost an hour and then cheat me on the tax amount". My husband just stood up and looked at me like "Don't do it. Just let it go". No wonder she is so rich. If you spit on people and pester them long enough, they will give in just to get rid of you.

UNWANTED SALES ADVICE

The rest of the day went like this. One nut case of an ugly lady came in and started correcting my dialogue. I ask if she liked Chico's and her response was, "Don't ever ask a question like that. It gives the customer a chance to say no and you lose a sale." I just stood there. What a shithead was my first thought. Her next remark was, "Is size ten the new large? Your sizes are all wrong. You need to get your store straightened around." My next thought was, she is not a shithead, she is a total jackass and I will just stare her down. Well that was wasted time. She rummaged through the store like a beggar looking for food in a dumpster. My poor husband saw that I was about to lose my temper and my mind, so he stood up and said, very firmly, "Do you need any help destroying the place or do you want to do it by yourself?" She looked totally shocked and very surprised a man was in the shop. His desk sits in back behind the last garment rack. It was placed that way so he could watch the front door and see what is going on. She stomped out the door without saying a word. Last we saw her, she was going into the cupcake store a few doors down. My husband said, "Well, I guess she is going down there to help them straighten out their business." I looked at him and said, "Don't think so". I think she went in to raise a little hell with them, since she was cut off at the pass here.

PHANTOM OF THE OPERA

$\mathcal{A}$round 3:00 this afternoon, the door opened and in came a mother and her two daughters. They were very nice. The girls were high school and college age. They were vacationing here from Washington DC. Very, very nice family. They were here all week for a beach vacation. The oldest girl tried on a coat that had been custom made in Paris. It came in from one of our Canadian consignors. She had brought in clothes that were very expensive and very new. She had two black velvet coats with pleated hoods and they were reversible. They were so far out expensive that we figured it would take a long time to sell them. These clothes needed just the right person to come in and buy them. The consignor had them made specifically for the Opera she attended. She called them her "Opera coats". Even the buttons on these coats were custom made. We knew it would take someone that lives in NY or another Canadian that was filthy rich to appreciate these coats.

When the young lady put on the coat her mother stated she looked like she belonged in "Phantom of the Opera". Her mother then put on the other black coat and they declared they wanted them both. I had to suppress my amazement because they were standing there in shorts and flip flops and old T-Shirts. We got to talking and the mom told me that she felt very fortunate that she had come into a lot of money and she felt very bad about how people were suffering with the way the recession was hitting the middle class. She then declared what wonderful democrats we are and what dumb asses the Republicans are. She told us that she works for the government and has a really good job. She and both of her girls had a great attitude and wonderful manners. It was the hi-lite of our day to visit with them. They left with four huge bags of clothes, coats and shoes. As they were leaving, they were trying to figure out how to pack all the new clothes in their little suitcases. The younger one told them not to worry; she could handle anything since she got her phantom of the opera coat. They left happy.

BLIND BUYERS

Sometimes when we think we have seen it all, here comes another weird story. Around 11:00 on a Tuesday morning, two ladies came in with canes for the blind. They both seemed to be having a hard time seeing the merchandise. They would use their canes to get around the garment racks. They tried on clothes for over an hour and then they worked their way up to the jewelry counter. They would pick up things and hold them right up to the end of their nose to see it. Bracelets, necklaces, earrings. Pick it up and hold it to the end of the nose and look at it sort of cross-eyed. It was kind of strange because it was like they had been in the store forever and touched everything and selected nothing. They must have tried over thirty outfits. Nothing fit, wrong material, too heavy, too long, too short, you know the usual complaints. Finally after going through three large trays of costume jewelry, one of them found a pair of beaded earrings priced at $2.00. They loved them, the color was great, but oh no wait, "Oh rats", one yelled, "There is a flaw in one of them". "A flaw, where I ask?" "Right there they pointed out'. I had to get the jewelers glass out to see it. I could not see it with the naked eye. I looked and looked and finally I saw what they were talking about. It was one zillionith the size of a pin head.

I could not believe it. I told them I could not find it with my eyes. One of them snapped, "Well we found it and want a discount". I had to ask how in the world with their bad eyesight they could see a flaw that small. Neither had an answer. "Sorry Charlie, no discount, but I will commend you on finding such a tiny flaw. You two are very special people to have found something like that". The last we saw of them, they were using their blind sticks tapping along the sidewalk and headed to the competitor down the street. Thank God and Greyhound. Nope that was not the last we had seen of them. They came back the next day and asked if we wanted to host a fashion show for their club that consists of people that have vision problems. My husband was in back at his desk and when he heard their request, he walked up front and said very matter of factually, "How in the world would partially blind people really enjoy a fashion show?" Total silence. We all just stood there. The two women stunned by his question. We were waiting for their answer. All we got was, "Well, it doesn't hurt to ask, does it?" "Nope", was my husband's reply, "And it does not hurt me to answer with an absolutely not. Good day ladies!!"

SCORE ONE FOR THE BEER TRUCK

Never a dull moment. One afternoon, I gathered the trash to put in the can by our back door. I opened the door and what greeted me was a surprise. There was yellow police tape all over the alleyway blocking it off and there were heavy wires lying on the ground. I called my husband to the back door to look and he said, "Hummm, looks like a large beer truck or the garbage man tore the wires off the building and the pole. Don't worry they will send someone out later to fix it". Next day the wires were still on the ground. We called the power company and they came out and said, "Not our lines, not our problem. Try Comcast". Next day we made 7-8 calls to Comcast. They kept transferring us and we got disconnected. Now we are into this thing for a week and no deliveries can be made around the back of the building. We figured the restaurants or bars down the alley way would call and get this problem fixed. No such luck. After almost two weeks, we called City Code Enforcement. He came out and told us the wires were not the power line and not Comcast. He did not know who they belonged to. He also told us that the building had been damaged and the gutter ripped off when the wires came down.

We asked him to tell the florist next door since she was not speaking to us. She is still mad about taking down her rain barrel. He went over there and told her and she came out the back door talking on her cell phone to her jeweler friend, telling him that we said there was damage to the building and there was not any damage. She just kept walking and talking and jabbering and we kept pointing up to the gutter that was dangling. She flipped her nose up and walked into her shop and slammed her back door shut. I called the landlord and asked her to send someone out to check the damage. She said that she got a call from the florist saying there was no damage. I assured her there was damage and she sent the repair man out to fix it. The florist is in her 50's and acts like she is a spoiled teenager. She always dresses like a sixteen year old and always has her pants so tight that they are up her butt crack. We decided that is her problem. She is dressing all wrong and it makes her miserable.

We found out later the wires were ripped out when a large beer truck was coming through the back alley. He put out yellow tape to let people know, but didn't bother to have it repaired.

CONSIGNMENT SHOP MUSICAL CLOTHES

Well it is almost the end of the week and time for the ladies that move their clothing from one consignment shop to another to bring their tired clothing in. A couple of them are so thoughtless they don't even remove the tags from the other shop. We know the routine. We call it "musical clothes". When we see them coming, we just tell them if the other shops can't sell it, neither can we. A couple of them just don't give up. I have gotten to the point where I meet them at the door and tell them to take the things to the trunk of their car and deliver the items to Goodwill. They can get a donation credit that way. I even called from the curb that they will not go to waste, that things that are that worn out get sent to a third world country. One of the shallowest remarks I have ever heard as a response to my Third World Country statement was this, "Why in the world would they want to give perfectly good clothes to poor people?" I never cease to be amazed with some of the attitudes of the people that come through our door.

COMPETITOR IN THE HOUSE

I left to pick up our lunch after a very busy morning. When I returned, my husband said that a competitor from across town came in and looked over our place. She spent almost $100 and told him she was looking for a place here in the Village to open another consignment shop. Good Luck!! Her prices are so high that you would not even know it is a consignment shop. She sells her place as a franchise and that makes the new owner have to mark prices up to cover the franchise fees. A few days later a couple came in and the woman was looking at everything and the man pulled out a camera and started taking pictures of our shop. We were very busy and had people lined up at the cash register. I heard my husband ask why he was taking pictures. The guy rushed out of the shop and before I could get around the counter and to the front door they were both gone. We have a pretty good idea why they were taking pictures. A week later they were setting up a shop one street over. I had better not see our pictures on their web page. Welcome to the business world and welcome to weirdo world. Their shop closed after four months in business.

DRESSING ROOM MIX-UP

My husband told me a story that happened while I was running a couple of errands. He had two very elderly ladies come in and start to pick out clothes. He hung their things in separate dressing rooms. About an hour into selecting things they decided to try on clothes. He saw them start into the wrong dressing rooms. He tried to tell them that they were in the wrong rooms, that they had them backwards. They were very deaf and somewhat senile. They could not understand what he was telling them. They went in and tried everything on and came out saying, "I just don't understand. Nothing fit. Not one thing. I picked out all my sizes". He pointed to the clothes and took them off the dressing room hooks and switched them around and said, "Now these are your clothes and these are your clothes. Try them on". They did and bought most everything they tried on. We don't think they ever figured out what was going on. Oh well, at least they left happy.

BEATUIFUL COATS

$\mathcal{I}$ thought we had seen it all, but today was at the top of our list. A lady walked in the front door carrying three beautiful coats. She hung them up on the rack for me to inspect. That day we had brought our little three pound Yorkie dogs to play in the back of the store for a couple of hours. While I was inspecting the beautiful coats, I was beginning to get a whiff of pee odor. I thought Oh, No, that is unusual, Baby Girl and Baby Boy always pee on the pad we place on the floor back there. What in the world is going on? At first I did not put two and two together. Here we have a full length black Diamond mink coat, a Burberry full length lined rain coat and a Ralph Lauren full length winter Cashmere coat. I reached up to open the beautiful mink coat and man alive, what hit me was the strongest eye watering odor of pee you can ever imagine. I opened the other coats and lo and behold the odor was horrible. I could not believe there was cat pee sprayed all over the coats. I closed the coats and looked at her with my eyes and nose burning and ask very nicely, "Do you have a cat?" Her reply, "Oh yes I do, how did you know. I have Floppsy and Moppsy and they sleep in my closet. I can't believe you knew I had cats". I said, "You have to get these coats out of the store right now. They are covered with cat pee. Your cats not only sleep inside the closet, they pee all over everything". "No way", she says firmly. "Oh yes", I reply, "Just open the coats and look at the pee spray all over them".

Well she was amazed. She took the coats to her car. She came back into the shop and told me, "She was very sorry that she had no idea they had wet on the things". In the next breath she said, "She had taken them to the cleaners and he told her there is no way to get cat urine off of clothes once it has been on there so long". I said, "Do you hear what you are saying. If you knew they had pee on them, why did you think we would take them?" "Well, I didn't know", she said, "I thought it was worth a try. Can you take my dresses if I check them out first?" "No way, no how. If the cats live in your closet do you think they are just avoiding your dresses? My husband has asthma. He is starting to wheeze just listening to this conversation". She finally left and I washed up from head to toe and then drove home and changed clothes and put my things in the washer. Man, people are really blind when it comes to their pets.

CAT DISCRIMINATION

A young lady about 5 feet tall, came rushing in carrying a load of clothes. She had on a tennis skirt and tennis panties up above her butt cheeks and a skimpy little top. She did not appear to be very clean. In fact, she was pretty dirty looking and driving a new Mercedes convertible. She rushed in and hung her things on the rack and yelled, "I have lots more; I will be right back. They are in the car". I started looking at the things she brought in and right off the bat, I saw cat hair. She came rushing back in and before she hung the next arm load on the rack I asked her, "Do you own a cat?" "Yes, Yes I do. As a matter of fact I have two cats". I had enough for one day. I blurted out, "I cannot take your clothes, we do not accept clothes from cat owners. Too many of our customers, including my husband and I, are allergic to cat dander. I am very sorry but please take your clothes back to your car." WoW!! Those were fighting words. She grabbed her things and yelled, "You are unbelievable. You are discriminating against cat owners. I will just take them to your competitor down the street". I went crazy and yelled, "Good luck with that". My husband got up from his desk and walked to the front door and watched as she screeched her Mercedes tires to the store five doors down. She stomped in there carrying her clothes and not one minute later she stomped back out carrying her clothes and screeched out and left the area.

Whew!! Out of sight out of mind. My husband got a real kick out of that little stunt. I was at the register checking out two ladies and one of them said, "Thank you so much for not taking clothes from that lady. She really did not look clean. Your shop smells so nice and everything is so clean we really appreciate the way you take care in selecting your consignors." A lady trying on shoes said, "Amen to that. I come here all the time because I know things are nice and clean. I was wondering if you were going to take her clothes. I should have known you wouldn't. Your shop is too clean for consignors like that. I also appreciate you asking if they have cats. I am very allergic to cat dander and some of the consignment shops around here don't care how dirty things are. They just want clothes to sell".

MAKE ME A PROMISE

Oh boy, it was almost 5:00 and closing time. We were both worn out. We started to close up and before we got the front door locked, in walked this very slim attractive blonde. I greeted her and she said she just wanted to try on shoes. She tried on several pairs of shoes. She looked a little tipsy while she was walking around trying them on. I kept thinking they look a little small, but it's her feet, she should know what size she wears. She stumbled over to the handbags and brought two pairs of shoes and a handbag to the checkout counter. Boy, did she reek of booze. I got her checked out and off she stumbled to the bar next door. Next morning we came in and were opening up and here she comes carrying those shoes. She was grinning from ear to ear. Her request was, "Could you re-consign these shoes for me? They are way too small and they kill my feet". I told her of course we could. Her next request was, "Please make me a promise. Don't let me buy any shoes from you when I have been drinking. I always do dumb things like that. Just tell me to wait until I am sober". Again we thought we had seen and heard it all.

GOLD ON GRIZZLY BEAR

Today is the beginning of a new week. We never know what the day will bring. We opened the store at 10:00 AM and got all set up and here comes our first customer of the day. It is a lady very, very tall and very, very big and ugly. She reminded us of a linebacker for the Green Bay Packers. Her hair was frazzled, her clothes were rumpled and she looked as if she had not bathed in weeks. She came dragging in clothes that were "rode hard and put up wet" as we used to say in Texas. I started looking through her things and picked through with two fingers. At the bottom of the stack of rags she brought in I found two beautiful Brighton handbags. I grabbed them up and handed her a consignment agreement to sign because she had BO so bad it was gassing up the entire room. I told her I could take the two bags and nothing else because the clothes were too worn. That was fine with her. The entire time she was standing there she was scratching her back with a big hair comb. She gathered up everything and before she left, she stated that her back was really itching. Before I could say, "OH MY GOD, she is not really doing that is she?" She walked over to the freshly painted wall of our beautiful dressing room and started scratching her back on the corner molding board. She looked like a large grizzly bear scratching against a tree, only here she is in my beautiful little consignment shop bumping and grinding and scratching so hard that the next thing we heard was a loud crack and she gathered up her things and walked out the front door.

When she was out of sight, we both looked over at each other and said, "That didn't just happen did it?" She had cracked the trim board from top to bottom. Split it wide open. We did not see her again for two months. She came in one day and we both wish we had seen her coming and locked the front door and slapped out the closed sign. This was the kicker. This, large and not so lovely grizzly bear of a woman, was dripping in gold and diamonds. Still stinking of BO and clothes, dirty and wrinkled. She wanted to leave a horrible outfit with us before she left for the summer to go to her house in the Hamptons. I mean she was weighted down with huge diamonds and gold chains and bracelets. Maybe a dozen on each arm and more than that on her neck. Big Diamonds! Big chunks of Gold! We were both stunned. When she left we looked at the local address she had given us. It was in the richest area of town right on the beach. Probably, a $5 million dollar house. Man who would have thunk It !!!!

LITTLE GREEN BUGS

The month of August brought us some very interesting characters. One morning after opening the store, a little old lady came through the front door with clothes on hangers and in very old plastic bags.

She wanted me to look at them to see if I could consign them for her. I could already give her the answer,

"No Way" but I decided to humor her and be very nice. I lifted the plastic and immediately saw small little green bugs all over them. I grabbed the bottom of the bag and tied it and started to the front door telling her, "That I had to get them out of the store because there were some kind of bugs all over them". She was very old and very slow to react. "Bugs?", she asked, "What kind of bugs?" I wanted to yell, "what the hell difference does it matter what kind of bugs, they are bugs and I don't want them in my shop".

I grabbed the clothes and raced out the front door and she followed very slowly. She finally got out to the sidewalk and I handed her the clothes. She said, "Well for goodness sakes, these things are brand new." I said, "Maybe you need to check your closets for bugs and critters". Her reply, "Must have picked them up at the place I bought them". She must have thought I was stupid or else she lost track of time. The tags were at least twenty years old and all rotten and sticking together. At least she did not make a big fuss. Just drove off very slowly. One of those seniors that needed to give up her drivers license ten years ago.

ROSARY BEADS

A little later that day, a young lady came running in the front door and wanted to know if I carried Rosary beads? I told her no, I had never had anyone come in to consign anything like that. She leaned over the jewelry counter and whispered, "I have got to find some right now, I mean today. I did something bad last night and I may be pregnant and I have to use those beads to help me get out of this. My mother will kill me."

I just stood there like, "And I thought I had heard it all look on my face." She asked if I knew any place that carried them. I said, "No I am not Catholic. The best place would probably be your church". Her reply as she flew out the door. "Man, I am not going anywhere near there right now."

HAMMER TOE AND BUNIONS

My life just gets more and more interesting. I am in the store by myself and an elderly man came riding up on a bike. He enters the store and says, "I am looking for tennis shoes for my girlfriend. They have to be a certain kind because she has two hammer toes and bunions". Oh man, I can't wait to see what this woman looks like after he described her feet. He stayed about an hour and he finally found a pair of shoes that might work for her. He asked for two pieces of copy paper. He also needed a writing pen or pencil. He took the shoes and traced around them and then he stood on the papers and announced that those might work. He was taking the papers back home to her and getting her to stand on them for a few days to see if they hurt her feet.

He asked if I would hold the shoes for a few days. I agreed. Four days later here he comes and announced that the shoes did not hurt her feet and she would pick them up on Saturday when she got paid. I really want to see this woman. Saturday came and right after we opened, in she came looking for those tennis shoes. Didn't even try them on. She just told us they fit perfect after she had tried them on using that paper he traced for her. I am speechless. She is just a short little dumpling with gray hair and sweet as she can be. She was very, very happy to have found shoes that fit. Just when I think we have heard it all! Glad it is Saturday and we will have a couple of days off.

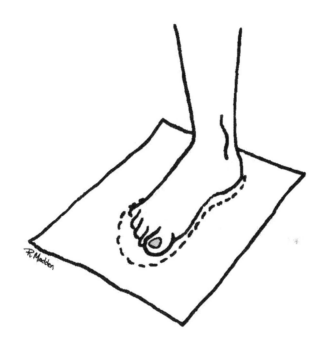

The perfect fit

TRAVELING ANTS

Tuesday we came in and opened the shop. The day was going pretty well with no weird happenings until around 2:00. A very, very, old man came in and said his wife had passed away and he wanted to consign her clothes. He asked if I would walk out to his car and look at the things before he brought them in. "Certainly", I told him. I opened the back car door and I swear I am telling the truth. He had ant mounds all over the back seat of his car. Ants were crawling all over everything. I slammed the door shut and told him to take everything to a dumpster and then take his car and have it detailed to get the ants out of it. I tried to show him the ants but he did not believe me. He just got back in the car and drove off very, very, slowly. I am allergic to fire ants, so I spent the rest of the day scratching and looking myself over to see if any ants were on me.

HUGE ANNOUNCEMENT

Same day, but late in the afternoon, a friend of mine stopped by. She held the front door open and announced to a store full of shoppers that she had just heard that a new goodwill store had opened out on "The Island" where all the rich people live. I was at the back of the store and she was yelling all this wonderful news from the front of the store. She yelled, "I am headed out there now and I will let you know about all the good buys I find". I could have strangled her. I did not even respond. She just let the door close and took off. I gasped to my husband "OMG, I cannot believe she just did that to us. What a thoughtless stupid thing to do to a friend." My husband very calmly looked at me and said, "Ha!! I have been telling you for a long time that she is not your friend. She is very jealous and self-centered, and I have another startling bit of information for you. Those are her good traits. You want me to list the bad things about her?" I dropped her like a hot potato. I was waiting for her to come back in with all her treasures from the second-hand store out on "The Island". She never came back. Thank God. You would have had to pull me off of her. With that announcement it was time to close the doors for the day.

ROTTEN HANGERS

Another day, another dollar or another nutty consignor. It was the end of the work week and I was cleaning and running the sweeper so I would not have to do it on Tuesday when we come back in. I had just finished when a woman came in and brought clothes to consign. She hung them on the rack and started tearing the plastic bags off them. Dust or something was flying through the air. I started looking at them and realized the foam lining on the hangers was rotten and falling apart. It was like dust and ashes flying everywhere. Please remember, I had just finished cleaning and dusting. Here is this shit flying throughout the shop. She saw what was happening and just stood there and shook the clothes piece by piece. I kept saying, "I can't take these clothes, they are too old". She kept insisting they had been cleaned and on hangers only a month or so. "No way", I said. "The hangers are falling apart". She still stood there and continued to shake the clothes. What a mess. It ended up with me being snotty and telling her I had just cleaned and she just undid everything I had just done. She did not care. Her only concern was to get me to take her clothes.

I did not, and she was pissed royally and left dragging her clothes behind her. It took me another two hours to clean up the dust and mess she had made. Made me wonder what I am doing in this business.

"Can it be possible that I am crazier than the consignors?" This day ended with a woman running into the store to find a certain color of scarf. She dug through everything we had in the store and then said

"Oh well, I know I can find one at the other consignment shop. I just wanted to give you a try." She walked out the door and as she was leaving a customer said, "Trust me you will find their prices much much higher." She shot back, "I don't think so, but thanks anyway. I was just trying to give a new shop some of my business." "OK", the customer said, "But they are really way high on everything." She took out the door and headed for the other consignment shop with an uppity attitude. My customer looked at me and grinned and said, "You watch, she will be back in a few minutes." I thought, "Yeah Right!!" Not five minutes later, here she comes flying in like a bat out of hell. Flew through the shop and grabbed three scarves and paid for them and left. Not a word, just left. My customer did the "Told you so dance", and died laughing.

COUNTING HANGERS

Counting Hangers is what we named this day. A young woman came in and very carefully started tapping the top of each hanger like she was counting inventory. It was crazy looking. She started at the front rack and worked her way to the middle. I could not stand it. I finally walked over to her and asked if she needed some help. "Nope I know what I am doing. I am fast at looking for what I like". She never misssed a beat, just tap, tap, tap. On she went like she was counting the hangers. That went on for twenty minutes. I went over to her again and she never stopped tapping. I finally just started rambling on about how she really had a system to look at the clothing. I truly thought I could break her chain of thought and stop the tapping pattern she had established. I finally came to the conclusion that she was a spy from the other shop and she was counting my inventory. That is when I really got firm with her. I put my hand up over the next hanger she was about to tap and declared she was all tapped out. "I have nothing that you would be interested in, please go tap somewhere else. You are disturbing my other customers" Believe it or not she never missed a beat. She finished up the last rack and left. Maybe she was one of those obsessive compulsive kooks that counts everything over and over. Just go do it somewhere else.

SNIFFING LEATHER

 am to the point now where I think it can't get any crazier. Wrong!!!
The store is full of people and I have a man standing in line sniffing
a Coach bag he had taken off the designer rack. He wants to buy it for
his wife, but it had to be the real thing. She will know if it isn't. He said
she told him she can sniff out a fake.

I guess he took it literally because he was waiting for us to check him
out and he was standing there in front of all these women sniffing this
Coach bag. Everyone was staring at him "like are you serious?"

"What in the world are you doing"? This was a candid camera
moment. I wish I had a security camera to capture this moment. You
could hear him sniffing that bag all through the store. It was like a hound
hunting a bone. Sniff, Sniff, Sniff.

Can you
smell a fake?

DRIVE THRU CONSIGNMENT SHOP

We are into September now and business is always slower in September. The snowbirds are gone and the kids are all back in school. It is the slowest month of the year for most business people in Florida. We expected things to go peacefully until Thanksgiving when the tourist and snowbirds return.

"AAAWWW," September 23, 2011 a day we will not forget. We had a steady flow of customers all morning.

Around noon, we had six ladies that came in together. They bought a few items and left the shop. The store was empty, so I went home to make our lunch. I had no sooner left than my husband called me to come back to the shop, something real bad had just happened. When I got back to the shop I saw a car sitting inside the shop. I walked through the yellow crime scene tape to find my poor husband trying to comfort the old lady that was driving. She was saying over and over, "I just want to kill myself, I just want to kill myself." My husband looked at my face and said very firmly, "Go to the back of the store and wait until the cleanup crew gets here. Go, Go, Go, Now". He saw the words ready to come out of my mouth as she said again, "I just want to kill myself." My first thought was, "Let me help you because you have just put me out of business".

Can you imagine all we had already been through and then she pulls up to park in front of our shop and she hits the gas instead of the brake. She tore out the entire front of the store and my husband said it sounded like a bomb going off. The big round Mercedes logo that sits on the front of the hood sheared off and flew through the shop. After all the emergency crews left, he saw it on the floor in front of his desk. He picked it up and said, "Well she is not getting this back." "Now why would you want that piece of crap. It is just a reminder of this nightmare." "Not really". he replied. "I am thinking of putting it on a big gold chain and wearing it around my neck as a memento" "OK." I said, "But you need a gold tooth in front to go with it". Anyway back to him standing out front beside a torn up chair she had hit and her sitting there whining about killing herself. A police officer walked up and gave her a ticket for $169. Yes folks, that is all the penalty she had to pay. The officer told her she probably would not get her license back. That made her even more unhappy.

About that time her daughter drove up in an even bigger Mercedes and said, "Well mom, when you do it you do it up big, don't you?, Not to worry, we will go rent you a car and you can finish your shopping".

Not one word about how sorry that they are for tearing the building up or anything thanking us for taking care of her until she got there. Just let's go rent you a car. Off they went. We could not believe it.

How cold and uncaring. They did not care about what it had done to our business. That was a prime example to me about what money does to people. They live in the richest part of Sarasota.

The landlord sent a cleanup crew over and four hours later we were running our shop behind plywood walls. It was the worst two months of our business life. It was like working in a plywood box with a small wooden door. Our business went down to half what it was. It took eight weeks to get the new doors and windows installed and almost five months to get the woman's insurance to settle with us. The worst part was not being able to see out the front because we were a little afraid someone else would decide to make our business a drive thru. The day they brought the doors and windows to repair the storefront, I mean the very minute they were installed, people started coming back in and shopping. Sad to say this was probably a blessing in disguise. Our business has grown and been better than we ever expected. I placed a large ad in the local newspaper to announce "Grand Re-Opening".

The ad read like this:

"We NOW have new windows,

We NOW have new doors,

Please don't drive thru our store anymore."

We both hope the very old woman with the very large Mercedes would be the first person to read our ad.

We hope the daughter was the second.

R. Madden

MY HUSBAND IS AN ANIMAL

This is Saturday and we are very busy. People are lined up to pay for their things. A lady walked in the front door and declared, "My husband is an animal. He is just an animal." She has on a full length mink coat, it was 90 degrees outside. She said, "I have to sit down. I have to eat at a certain time, I have to go to the bathroom at a certain time and I have to drink at a certain time". OMG, there is no time to mess with this Kook. She heads for one of my three dressing rooms and sits down and starts looking through her bank bag that she is carrying. It is full to the brim with money. Scared us to death because it looked like several, several thousand dollars. Now the ladies that come into our shop are not really well off and we did not want anyone tempted to snatch her bank bag. I told her to zip it up and put it under her arm. She did and then got up and started carrying shoes from the rack to the counter and dragging clothes off the hangers and stacking them on the counter. I tried to play like this was just a normal way to shop but it was hard because she was not bringing pairs of shoes, just one shoe each and it was confusing people trying to look at the shoes. Her dog was all over the place and she kept saying, "I have to sit down, I have to eat at a certain time and drink and go to the bathroom at a certain time". as she was dragging clothes off the rack and over to the counter. I was ready to tell her to stop when a horn started honking out front, a very loud non-stop honking. She declared, "He is just an animal, if I don't go out he will come in and he is mean as hell." I ordered her to go out and tell him to stop honking or I would. She said, "No one tells Jay what to do. He will honk until I go out there." I yelled, "Get out there then". She continued to tell everyone how he is mean to her.

Now I pictured Jay to be a huge tough looking business type person since she told us he was a retired doctor. I went to the back of the shop to get more merchandise bags. The bags were on the bottom shelf. As I raised up with the bags in my hand, I could see my husband motioning to me and I was saying to this nutty woman, "I would not put up with that crap. I would rip him a new one and he would not talk to me that way ever again". I turned around and was facing this dried up little old man with two walking canes and a sour look on his face. I am sure he heard me. I yelled, "Well, hello there, you must be Jay. Your wife has been telling us what a nice person you are. You are even better looking than she described you to be." He told her to go get in the car and she did and he hobbled back out the front door. I will say it again, "What have I done to deserve an experience like this?" I hope we never see them again.

DEAD MAN AND DRUNK WOMAN

Early one morning before we left for work, we were reading the newspaper and drinking our coffee and watching the local news. We were just reading about a dead man found in the middle of the street two blocks down from our shop. They were not sure how he died. When we got to work and started our day, in came a police detective. He asks if we could identify the man in the pictures he was holding. It was pictures of the dead man and pictures of a man they suspect shot him at the ATM machine. Man, what a way to start the day. He declared we had a murderer running around this area and if we saw anything suspicious just give him a call. We agreed and he left. We looked at each other and I said "If the murderer walks in here, will you call the police?" "No way", was his reply. I said, "Even if the guy walks in the front door and says, "Hello folks, I am the murderer they are looking for?" "I still will not call the police!" he snapped. I said, "Why, because you are afraid, like me, that they will come in, guns blazing and shoot both of us and the murderer will walk out unscathed. "Yep, and their claim will be the mouthy little woman with the stupid Texas accent came at us with a bottle of Windex. The poor husband got in the line of fire trying to dive under his desk". End of story! "OK!, let's get back to work." A week later, they caught the murderer and we stopped worrying about getting shot.

Next thing we saw was a woman across the street lying on the ground in front of a bar. We could see her hair was very jet black long and thick. My husband called me up front to take a look at the woman and what was happening. The police were standing over her. My husband said, "Now I know why they named that bar "The Hair of The Dog." I just gave him a look like I can't believe you just said that and I went back to my dusting.

DRUG BUST BY HORSE

Lunch came and went and we had a fairly busy day. Just when you think things are a little dull, we looked out the front window and saw two mounted policemen on two huge, beautiful horses making an arrest in front of our store. They had the guy wedged in between the horses and they were talking to him. Then they opened the trunk of his car and pulled out a huge bag of white stuff. Guess what? Next thing you know they are handcuffing him. This seems very minor and just a quick little arrest. Not so!! It took over three hours to get him processed and into a paddy wagon. I was standing there looking out the window and my husband came up front and asked me what in the world I was staring at? He said, "We got pictures to prove this really happened now what are you looking at?" My reply, "Do you not realize they have been standing there for over three hours and that one horse's rear end is pointed right over the sidewalk at the front door. I am very concerned he will let loose any minute now and we don't have a shovel up here. What would we do?" He started laughing and looked at me and said, "Only you would worry about something like that". They finally left and we got back to work.

DON'T YOU WANT TO SAVE A BUNDLE?

We are half way through the week and this has been a day we call "Clothes Kickers." You know instead of tire kickers, we have clothes kickers. Over and over the front door would open and ladies would just look and walk out. We have days like that every now and then. Then we have days where everyone that walks through the front door ask if we have any sales going. For crap sake, everything we have is on sale, we are a used clothing shop. We always reply, "Everything we have is on sale. We are a consignment shop". Boring but true! Well, today turned out to be another winner. A young lady in a business suit came strolling in and ask to see the owner. I told her I was the owner and she went into a canned speech about how her credit card machine would save me money. I told her I was very happy with what we used through our bank. That did not set well with her. She started saying in a loud voice, "Don't you want a better deal? Don't you want to save a bundle? The owner of our card company lives right here in Sarasota. He will personally help you with any problems you encounter". I told her again, "No thank you, I do not want to change at this point". Now she really got angry. "Fine," she said, "I just sold one of my machines to the cutest little shop a few blocks from here". Then she went on to give, a store full of my customers, the "cutest little shop's address." She stated what good buys they have there. I finally walked out from behind the counter and toward her and she left very quickly. What a stupid sales person. If I wanted to change in the future, she left no card for us to contact her. She only left us with a very bad impression.

TACKY LITTLE SWEATER

---

t is getting close to the holidays, we are taking in fall and winter items now. My friend Terri brought in a sweater that was a little ugly. It was a turtle neck sweater, long sleeves and made of something like silver and black tin foil. I asked her what price she thought I should ask. She said $15.00 because it is tacky. We checked it in and hung it on the sweater rack. The next day here comes one of the sales ladies from the other shop in the area. She is snooping around and came to this sweater. She took it off the rack and looked at the price and yelled at me, "Do you have any idea about designer pricing?" I said, "Excuse me!!!" She yelled again "Do you know anything about designer clothing?" This stupid woman did this in front of a store full of customers. I walked over and she pulled the label out and said, "Do you know who he is?" I was furious now at her rudeness and I yelled back, "Yes, I know who he is, he is the man that sells his designs to Target and K-mart and anyone that will buy them. I bought my little dog's designer basket from target and his name was on it". I yanked the sweater out of her hand and started toward her to back her out of the store. As she got to the front door, "I yelled every one of you women have been through my store and I have never nosed through your store". Her reply, "Well you should come over and look at our store." I snorted very hatefully, "I would, but I have no interest or desire to rummage through your store. I am only concerned with what is inside my front door and nothing outside those doors. I take care of my business and don't nose into other people's business".

She threw her nose in the air and stormed out. I cannot believe how "ballsie" these women are. I turned to my husband and I told him to watch they would send someone back to buy the sweater. I took the sweater to the back storeroom and left it there. Not three minutes later a weasel of a little man came rushing into the store and went right over to the rack where the sweater had been hanging. I walked over to the little skinny guy and ask, "If I could help him?" He said, "No, I am looking for something specific". "I asked, "What it would be". He said, "Oh, I will know when I see it!!!" I said, "We do not carry clothing for men". His response, "I know that, I am looking for something else". He looked all up and down the wall where the sweater had been. It took a minute but my husband and I looked at each other and realized the sales woman that just left after giving me the designer clothing lecture, went back, told her story and sent the owner's husband back to buy the sweater. I asked again if he needed any help, and he just turned and walked out. What a weasel thing to do.

Now my customers are coming in telling us that the owner of the other shop is saying that we are hurting her business because we are pricing things too low. Sorry but this area is not a high rent district. This neighborhood is middle-lower income and fixed income ladies looking for a bargain. The consignors know that and still bring their clothes to us. The competition carries designer bags some priced at $1,300. Right! and she and the bag have been in store the last 15 years. Who buys a bag that expensive in a consignment shop in a strip mall.

PETA Party

$\mathcal{I}$t is getting cooler now. It is almost November. We have been doing a very brisk business. We have a lady that is a member of PETA and would do almost anything or sell almost anything to protect animals.

She has consigned with us for the last 2 months. She picked our shop because we do not carry fur of any kind. She brings us beautiful designer clothing. She always comes to our shop when she gets her hair done next door. Today she came in and told me that she had walked to the shop that is our competition and opened the front door and told them she would not be consigning with them anymore because she found a friendlier shop and they do not sell any fur or fur lined clothing. She told us that story and then got in her car and left. No sooner had she left the lot than the sales woman down the street came stomping through the store with a customer in tow. I sighed and walked over to them and asked, "What they needed this time". "We are looking for a fur coat. My customer wants to buy a fur coat". I knew it. I knew it. How shallow and ridiculous they acted. Just picture two old ladies walking tiny little steps very fast through a small shop looking for an excuse to cause trouble. Both had glasses on a chain hanging from their neck, heads bobbing all over the place. Grey haired Mrs. Cravats type women. I told them we do not carry fur of any kind. The sales woman ran over and grabbed a silver coat and said, "This is fur". I calmly said, "Nope, it is fake from

Paris". She huffed, "Well you have it priced too low. Don't you know it is worth more than that?" I did not say a word, I just walked over and held the front door open and they left in a huff. What a picture. Two old women looking for a fight and did not get one. Now their best shot at me is to come in and take a lot of clothes off the rack and take them into a dressing room to check out the prices. They just walk out and leave a dressing room full of clothes for me to return to the rack. They have never bought anything.

HOLIDAY BASKETS TAKE FLIGHT

We are getting closer to the Holidays now and I wanted to hang out baskets with red poinsettias in them.

I was feeling like we needed to dress up the front of the store for Christmas. We went to a silk flower shop, bought two beautiful baskets to hang out on the front awning. We had forgotten how the tropical breezes come up very fast, even on beautiful sunny days. Here we go. We hung them out and within an hour the flowers had blown down the driveway. My husband went out and gathered them up and brought them in. The wind died down and we hung them back out. Same thing only this time they blew all the way down to the front door of the competition. My husband said he felt like they thought he was peeking in the windows because he kept bending over to pick up the flowers and his head was bobbing up and down along their front windows. After two weeks of hanging and chasing the flower baskets we gave up and sat them on the check-out counter.

GREASED BOOBS AND THE BURGER SHOP

few months ago we had a really successful little Irish pub shut down. We heard the owner's wife was very ill and he needed to take care of her. The place sat empty for almost four months and then a young couple from up north came in and renovated it. They are a very nice couple. Very friendly. Not married but been together for a long time is what they told us. We thought we would try to help them out by telling our customers to try lunch over at the Burger Shop. The first day they opened we ordered lunch and they got the order wrong. When we mentioned it the owner's girlfriend, she said, "Oh well we will to get it right next time." How weird. Not even an attempt to make it right. We let it go and kept telling people to try them out. Then we got the feedback. We have two ladies that come in every Thursday morning. Last Thursday they had lunch at the Burger Shop. They went in and were the only two people in the place and no one came over to take their order for almost 15 minutes. They said the owners girlfriend was talking on her cell phone and ignoring them. Then, when she finally came over they placed their order for hamburgers and fries and requested the burgers be well done. They waited another 45 minutes and finally out came the order. They looked at the meat and it was almost raw. They finally got her attention and told her they had asked for the burgers to be well done. She huffed at them, "Well if I had known you wanted them Burnt, I would have Burnt them". She yanked up the plates and took them back to the grill. She came back with charcoal burgers. They told her they could not eat them and she gave them the check. They paid and walked out. They told us they would never go back. We told them we felt really bad about recommending they have lunch there.

Something very important that I have left out. From the first time we met this couple we noticed the young lady had what appeared to be new store bought boobs. She wore very, very, low cut tops and it appeared she smeared grease on the boobs. It was very awkward to carry on a conversation with her. Those two huge things pointed right out there for everyone to see. Very awkward. The week they opened we had a nice couple come in and the lady bought a lot of things and her husband asked if we knew a good place to have lunch. We told them the Burger Shop is new and they might want to try it. Off they went. We did not know he is a food critic for the local newspaper. The next week when they were in our shop the wife told me that she was reading the newspaper food section one morning over her coffee and someone wrote an article rating the Burger Shop. She said on a scale of 1-10 this writer gave them a "2" overall.

She said she asked her husband what name he used when he was rating a restaurant and he told her. She looked and it was her husband giving them a very low rating. They both said the food was really awful and the service was worse. Again we had to tell them we were sorry we sent them over there. A couple of days later one of my customers came in and the store was crowded and she said she would wait because she wanted to tell me something important. Ten minutes later I walked to the back of the store where she was waiting to talk to me. She said she had ordered dinner for guests that were coming over last night. She picked the food up and got home and opened it. They started to eat and found the food was so bad they had to throw it away. They went out for fast food because everyone was hungry and the restaurants during snowbird season are all packed by 7:00. She went over to the Burger

Shop and was very nice in telling the young boob waitress how bad the food was that she had picked up the night before. The "boob waitress" looked at her and said, "Well, I ate it and it was very good". With that she turned around and left my friend standing there. Trust me we will never send anyone over there again.

Late in the afternoon the front door flies open and in walks the "boob waitress". She headed straight for my husband's desk, with her large greased boobs leading the way. She leaned over his desk and proclaimed the restaurant would be changing their hours. They would only be open for dinner at 4:00 in the afternoon. Poor thing he just kept looking at his computer screen. She left and I snapped "I really don't appreciate her coming in my shop with her greased up boobs and sticking them in your face." He looked at me like, I tried not to look but they were just out there bouncing around. A few days later there was a sign on the door that said they were closing for good. We had good intentions; they just did not have good food. Burger Shop is gone. I told one of my friends about how she leaned over my husband's desk with her greased boobs sticking out. My friend screeched "Oh My God! He is 84 years old, was she trying to kill him?"

MUG SHOT MOM

ell we are into December now and people need Christmas money. They bring in everything they can just to make some money for gifts. A mother and daughter came in one morning in early December and wanted to consign some Hollister shorts and shirts. I looked at them and could not believe how small they were. They were size zero and no more than 5-6 inches from waist line to hem. They looked like they were made for a Barbie doll. I told them I would try to sell them and then got them to sign an agreement like all our other customers sign. It says if they do not sell in 60 days you have 5 days to pick them up or they will be donated. They were tried on several times but always too small. Sixty days came and went and not one piece out of 20 items sold. I pulled them off the rack and placed them in the back for them to pick up. After two weeks I called to tell them they would be donated. The mother called and said they would be there next week to pick them up. A month passed and the shorts and tops were still back there. I tried to call and her voice mail box kept saying it was full and would not accept any messages. Next, we tried to email her and the email address was not good. I finally reached her voice mail and told her she had until Thursday to pick the things up. If they are not picked up by Thursday they will be donated. Guess what. Thursday came and went, so, on Friday they were donated. Saturday afternoon the daughter appeared in our shop in very skimpy clothes and said, "My mom told me you probably already donated them, but for me to stop by and see if the clothes were gone." I asked her last name and when she told me, I told her the shorts and tops left our place yesterday. She said, "Oh that is OK. We were late coming to get them anyway." She left. Ten minutes later the mother called yelling and screaming about us donating $300 worth of clothes. She was going to report us for running a shady business. Then she hung up on me after I reminded her agreement she signed said she would pick them up within 60 days. I was crushed because we did not have a mark or a complaint against us in any of the business's we had owned over 25 years. I was very upset because she was telling us that she was going to tell all her friends. I almost cried. My husband and a friend tried to comfort me. Nothing made me feel better. I just knew my business was doomed. A little while later and still not feeling any better about having an angry customer, my husband said come back here to my computer. I said, "Why?" "Because I think I found something that will make you feel much better about this whole mess". He turned the screen around and said here is Miss Shady business. There starring back at me was a mug shot of a trashy looking woman who had been arrested several times for DUI. I just stood there looking at her mug shot and then the next picture that came up was someone making fun of her saying she had a scary personality and ugly mug shot. What a wonderful example this woman was for her teenage daughter. And she was threatening to bad mouth me to her friends. What friends? The jailbirds around her. What a foul mouthed horrible person.

LET'S ALL ACT CRAZY

t is March 2012 now and we are headed to work hoping it will be a fruitful day. Or an uneventful day anyway. We pulled up in front of our shop and there sits the sister of the other shop owner.

I said, "What in the world is she doing now?" She looked at us and got out of her car and walked down the sidewalk to work at her sister's place. She left her car parked in front of my shop all day.

I was livid. Next day, the same thing. I was bitching and gripping and my husband said, "Just let it go.

She will move it when she decides she has ticked you off enough". She parked there for a week and the following week I had enough of her bullshit. She pulled up one morning just as we did. That was the final straw for me. My husband kept the windows up and kept telling me to stay calm and not say anything. We went into the shop and I put my purse down and there she was unloading her car and starting down the street to her sister's shop. I started to the front door and my husband started yelling,

"Don't go out there, don't you go out there". He just kept saying that. I ignored him and shoved the front door open and yelled, "Could you tell me why you keep parking in front of our shop"? She turned around like she knew it was coming and said, "Oh, I am just leaving our spaces open for our customers."

I walked right up to her and said "Oh, that is fine, We will just park in front of your sister's place and that way we will all be acting crazy. I will even ask our customers to park down there and walk back up here.

They would be glad to do that for us". She just stomped off and a few minutes later she came back and moved her car. She has not parked there since.

BREATHALYZER TEST

think I mentioned we are surrounded by little bars and restaurants. Sometimes the patrons leave their cars overnight and we have to put up with it. Usually it happens on the weekends and does not cause us a problem. Well we have had a large silver SUV parked in front of our building for over a week and no one has moved it. I finally called the city and they told me to call a tow truck. I did just that. They asked if I was in the Village area and told me, "That I would have to sign a form saying I was the one responsible for having this car towed". "I told them I would call my landlord". I ask the landlord if he would call and have the car towed. He said "No way. It is written or grandfathered in to the area that it is city parking and you cannot have anyone towed away". He said, "They can sue you and he would not take that chance." I could not believe it. I asked what I was supposed to do about this huge old SUV covering the front parking area of my shop. He told me to call the code enforcement guy. I did and he told me the same thing. I was really singing the blues to him by now and he looked up who the car belonged to and gave me the owner's name and address. He told me the best thing to do would be to mail him a letter. He said, "Wait a minute there is a reason the guy can't move his car. It has a breathalyzer on it and he can not drive it when he has been drinking". Oh crap just what I needed to hear. My husband typed a letter telling him if the car was not moved by the next day we would call a towing company. We were going to mail it but

I decided to drive it over to the address that the car was listed under. It was only about six blocks away. I put the letter in an envelope and drove over to his house. It was a little scary because it was very run down and it looked like he had hit the garage door a few times. I got up the nerve to ring the doorbell and I could hear a gravelly voiced old woman yelling, "John, come answer the front door". "OK, mother", he yelled. About that time the door flung open and there stood a really hard mean looking old guy about 65, very big and very gruff. I told him, "I was delivering a letter to someone named John and that I needed him to move his car right now". Trust me this guy looked like he just got out of prison. Very rough looking, like "Rode Hard and Put up Wet" type person. He said "Oh he is my roommate. I will give him the letter". I rushed back to the car and locked the doors and pulled out of the driveway. I was shaking. That was a little scary. I stopped by the house because it is on the way back and just as I got in the door, my husband called and said a really big scary looking guy just rushed across the parking lot and moved his car. I could not believe it. He told me that story about having a roommate and he must have run all the way up there and picked up his car. I don't think I will be doing anything else like that again. It could have been really ugly.

PATCHOULI PERFUME

When we entered the front door this morning the phone was ringing. It was a lady that was interested in bringing her clothes in for consignment. I went over our policy with her and she said she would be there right after lunch. We were very busy all morning and did not have time to stop for lunch. Around 1:00 the front door opened and a large rather loud lady comes in carrying an arm load of clothes. No sooner had she entered the front door when we were all over come with a horrible sweet pungent odor of perfume. She walked over to our front counter and Oh boy, the odor was coming from her. There were about 5 or 6 customers in the store and they were all looking like they had just been gassed. They were staring at her and sniffing and covering their noses. In between gasps for fresh air I managed to ask her what brand of perfume she is wearing. "Oh, my gosh, thank you for noticing. It is Patchouli oil and I love it". By now my eyes are watering and my husband had gone to the double doors in front and propped them open. It filled the room so fast that that was not enough relief, so he rushed to the back door and propped it open. Not even fear of a vagrant wandering in could stop him from opening the back door to our alley. Not even fear of a would-be robber could keep him from letting some breathable air into our building. I leaned over her clothes and the odor of her wonderful Patchouli nearly knocked me over. I thought how in the world am I going to tell this woman her clothes smell worse than shit. We would rather smell backed up sewer than that God awful odor of sweet overbearing perfume.

She was just going into the part telling us that she makes a special trip to Whole Foods to buy this oil.

She told us that she puts it all over her body after she showers. I was standing there thinking, "And you have not passed out yet?" By this time most of the customers had left or they were just overcome by this imitation mustard gas. There is no other way to describe the odor, but just call it lethal. With tears in my eyes and my nose running profusely, I explained we did not accept clothes that carry a perfume odor.

"Oh, but this is one all my friends like". "I am sorry", I told her, "But the perfume odor is too strong to put your clothes in our shop". She just kept saying, "This is ridiculous, everyone loves my perfume". I told her a very nice thing she could do would be to give her clothes to her friends that like her perfume so much. Finally she gave up and gathered up her smelly clothes and left. The odor was still in the building so we had to work the rest of the day with all the doors open. Right before closing time a little old lady came in the front door, sniffed the air and said, "Oh my Lord, someone is wearing Patchouli perfume". People used to wear that awful stuff back in the fifties. I hated it then and I hate it now. Worst stuff I ever smelled. It takes forever to get the odor out of your nose." We laughed and told her that was why the doors were propped open. She was a hoot. She told us it might take a few days for the odor to go away. It took three days before we could breathe without that sweet odor knocking us over. This may have been a nice perfume in a much smaller application.

CUPCAKES

Some days when business is slow we watch out the front window to see how many huge, oversized SUV'S with large and lovely sized women and their children pull up and go into the Cupcake place. It is always interesting to watch them go in and come out eating a large cupcake or carrying a big box of cupcakes out with them. We are not real fans of these cupcakes because sometimes they try to walk through our store eating them and they get them on the clothes or drop them on the floor. They are so loaded with butter and grease that it always leaves a big greasy spot on the floor. It takes 20 Mule team Borax and an act of Congress to get it out of the carpet. We finally put a sign on the front door saying "No food or drink Please". They still bring those grease balls in. When we see them coming we all start yelling, "HEAD EM OFF AT THE PASS." We meet them at the door and tell them we cannot let them come in with the grease balls. We always tell them how sorry we are but our consignors would have a fit if their clothes got stained. Most of the problems came from very large Mom's and equally large kids.

They show up at the front door with cupcake icing all over their hands and faces. Makes us cringe to think about it.

These are truly the most delicious "Heavenly Cupcakes" we have ever tasted. We always buy them for customer gifts. We are famous for taking cupcakes in place of wine, when we accept dinner invitations. Everyone loves them. We love them, just don't bring them into our shop.

CRAZY WOMAN AND CONTRABAND SHOES

few days ago one of our consignors's stopped by and wanted to consign a pair of Bandolino shoes.

She told us a story of how one of her crazy friend gave her the shoes and the next day got mad at her and called to tell her she wanted them back. She hung up on her and brought the shoes to be con- signed. We checked them in and tagged them and placed them out on the shoe rack. We knew exactly who the crazy woman she was talking about was. She is beyond crazy. She tried to bring in filthy, old torn and worn clothes and I kept turning them down. She was very, very rude and hateful the last time I told her, "Don't even open the bag because I can save us both time. I do not want them". She stormed out of the building and we have not seen her for months. HA!! Until today. Here she comes flying in the front door looking for the damn shoes. She grabs them off the shoe rack and starts yelling "These are my shoes. This woman stole them from me. These are mine". I walked over yanked the shoes out of her hands and stated, "These are not your shoes, these are consigned with us. They belong to one of my consignors." She yanked them back and yelled tell me, "Who consigned them?" "I will not. it is none of your business. Please stop yelling!" I was thinking, you crazy bitch get the hell out of my shop.

Luckily no one was in the store but a friend of ours. We had all been standing in the back laughing and visiting when this whirl wind from hell came charging into our place. My husband just sat there and watched all this unfold. He said later he just wanted see how I would handle this nut case without him having to get up out of his chair. I would not give her the name of the consignor, knowing it was exactly who she thought it was. I stated, "Do you have any idea how common these shoes are. There are thousands of the exact same shoe out there. These are not your shoes". Her comment, "Well, I will call the police and report you have contraband in your store. These shoes are stolen". I said, "Contraband WHAT?"

Then she had the nerve to put a bag of clothes up on the counter and tell me she wanted to consign them. I was flabbergasted!! I started yelling, "Out, out, out. You were so hateful to me last time you were in here, I cannot believe you even came through the front door again. Now please leave". She snapped, "I am going to report you have stolen shoes in your shop. I am going to call the police and file a report". "Go ahead and call the police and get a warrant to have the shoes arrested and taken into custody. Just get out". She got to the front door and yelled, "I am going to the police now but first I am going to consign these things with your competitor down the street.""That would be the proper thing to do", I said, "Because they are as crazy and mean as you are. Now shut the damn door and don't let it hit you in the back side." I walked to the back of the store and my husband was sitting there with his mouth open. My friend was dumbfounded. Her only remark was "Man, I never saw anything like that. You are always so nice. I didn't know you had that much fury in you. You handled that pretty well. You verbally roughed her up, didn't you?" "Yeah right", my husband said, "She just stopped short of throwing rocks and spitting on her."

BIRDS AND BROOM STORY

———————

We pulled up in front of the shop this morning and twigs and straws were laying all over the sidewalk in front of the doors. We got out and looked to see where it was coming from. There was a pigeon helping a sparrow build a nest right above our front door. My husband said very harshly, "We can't have that.

There will be bird crap all over the place. The front door is not the place for them to be building a nest".

We got in the front door and opened up and he headed to the back to get the broom. He went out front and knocked down the nest. A few minutes later we noticed straw and twigs droppings on the sidewalk again. Again he grabbed the broom and went out to discourage them from settling in above our front door. Again, an hour, later they were back up there and this went on all morning. Now there are two pigeons and one sparrow and this had become a royal battle between them and my husband and his broom. They were not giving up and he was not backing down. Later in the afternoon when we noticed no more twigs and no more straw falling on the sidewalk, he felt he had won the battle. We went about our business all afternoon and just as we were getting in the car to leave the jeweler yelled, "Hey, we watched you all morning fighting the birds out in front of your building. Guess what!!! The poor little bird was trying to build a nest to lay her eggs. She finally gave up and laid them out here on the sidewalk". Talk about feeling bad. My poor husband felt like a heel. We got in the car and I stated, "With the kind of luck we have, PETA would be out there tomorrow to picket our place". He just kept saying, "I am not a bird expert, how did I know it was a female bird. For all I knew it could have been two males shacking up together and what the hell was a pigeon doing helping a sparrow anyway?"

THE CROSS DRESSER

Here we are ready to start the day. The sun is shining, the sky is clear and all is right with the world. So we thought. For the last two weeks this very nice looking, very clean cut, and very well dressed young man has been coming in. He seems very shy and carries a very large backpack. He always looks for the silky, softer material. He also favors white or cream color. He wears a wedding band so we just figured he is married and shopping for his wife. WRONG!!!!! After his third trip to our shop, I decided to ask if he needed some help to find something. Keeping in mind he has never bought anything. I was really hell bent on finding out why I kept getting these strange vibes every time he walks in. I walk over to him and ask if he needs help finding anything. His reply, "No, not really". I must have lost my mind because I opened my mouth and out came the words. "You are shopping for yourself, aren't you?" He looked kind of surprised and answered, "Yes, and could I please try on some of the skirts and this white silk blouse?" When I finally took a good breath in, I told him, "Yes, and he could go to the first dressing room". He took the clothes and his huge backpack and closed the curtains to set about his hunt for a white silk outfit. Thank God and Greyhound there were no little old ladies around. After a few minutes he came out and asked if I could help him find a silk skirt with a larger waist. He loved what he tried on but the waist was too small. Before I knew it, "I was giving him the low down on how a man's waist was thicker and larger than most women". I explained, "That it would be very hard to find a waist just his size, since he was built like a man". Oh my Gauze, I had no idea what I was talking about. I just knew I was extremely uncomfortable and my husband was in dire straits at the front counter. His face was so red that I could not be sure if he was about to pop a cork and start laughing or he was just dying on the vine about to cry. I just know that I was trying to act like it was very normal like an everyday event for a man to come into my store and try on ladies' clothes.

He tried on a few more things, said he would be back later, and then he left. No sooner had he closed the front door than my husband busted out with, "What in the hells bells were you talking about? Men have bigger waist and then you told him about how much more comfortable he would be in a heavier material". I just stood there and finally I answered, "He is packaged a lot different than a woman, so I thought he needed more material to hid his packaging. Does that make sense?" I have never seen anyone laugh as hard as my husband after I explained the material thing. Every time he looked at me he started laughing again. Well, now I will just have to remember that material packaging thing the next time I go shopping for clothes. I stammered, "Give me a break would you? That stupid backpack was making me very nervous. He could have had a gun or knife or something lethal in it." My husband said, "Yeah like maybe a can of hairspray or tube of lipstick?" I told him, "No that I was serious, that I have seen news on TV where a serial killer carried a back pack and I was trying to be aware and alert for anything like that". I said, "I was truly nervous about how he acted". I also told him, "Serial killers look clean cut and neat like this guy". My husband's come back was, "Right you are about the clean and neat, but most serial killers don't go to a ladies consignment shop and try on ladies clothes before they murder someone". "Exactly the point I was trying to make", I told him, "He quite possible could be a serial killer that tried on ladies clothes before killing the owners husband with his silk stocking, therefore allowing the man's wife to leave the building unharmed. Now that is my story and I am sticking to it. Well when we decided that we had cleared up this whole tangled web, we went back work. We both agreed we would never see this guy again. Thank goodness!!!

THE RETURN OF THE CROSS DRESSER

Here we go again and here he comes again. This time he did not carry his backpack. He was carrying a fanny pack. Why in the devil is it called a fanny pack when people wear it in front at their waist? That is where he wore it and I could only imagine a switchblade or small hand gun or whatever. For some reason I freaked out and after I said good morning to him, I ran out the front door and down the sidewalk to the cupcake shop. I tore through the front door where the owner was sweeping and I yelled, "Come over quick. I have a cross dresser wearing a fanny pack looking for a silky blouse and his waist is too big for a skirt. I have a very bad gut feeling about him and I need you to come over fast and act like you are looking for something". I mean I was spitting this out so fast that her head was spinning and she was trying to take it all in. I turned and held the front door open and said please hurry. "OK", the lady cupcake store owner said, "I am right behind you." I ran like an antelope back down the sidewalk and grabbed the two front doors and propped them wide open, almost wrong side out. If he was going to get me, I wanted to be able to scream for help. There is a large auto repair shop directly across the street and I knew they would come running if we needed them. After I got the doors propped open, I gathered myself and walked back into the store. Right behind me was the Cupcake lady, broom in hand. Ready to swat anything. She flew through the front door and said, "I need a Lilly Pulitzer dress. We are working on a Lilly

Party and making cupcakes in those bright colors she uses. Do you have anything?" I very robot like said, "Oh yes, come back here and take a look at this dress". She grabbed the dress out of my hands and started waving it around like a scene out of the exorcist. She was waving the broom and waving the dress and talking fast because she was on a mission. The mission, to see how fast she could get this guy to run out of our shop. I ask her to help us and she was damned determined to do exactly that. I was so distracted by her dancing and waving the broom and dress that we never saw the guy leave the store. My husband finally yelled, "You all can stop the show now, Elvis has left the room".

VERY DRUNK LADY HAD A SERIOUS PROBLEM

Today had been very uneventful until around 2:00. Two ladies came in the front door and they were very, very, drunk. The older lady with the dyed black hair wanted to try on cocktail dresses. She picked out several that I could clearly see were going to be far too small for her. She was a size 16-18 and the dress she really liked was a size 8. The dress was a bright orange with layered ruffles over the entire bodice. It was a dress for a teenager, not a 60 year old that is a plus size. My husband and I could see what was about to happen. She went into the dressing room and emerged looking like a huge orange, ruffled snowman. It was just horrible. Her friend that she came in with was as drunk as she was. She asked her friend what she thought. "Does the dress look OK?" Her friend looked at her and said, "You look like a layered Halloween cake. Take it off. You look very fat and dumpy in that dress and orange is not your color. Take it off it is making me sick to look at it." Then the friend stumbled out the door and sat in the car waiting for her. Really she was hanging out the car window because she was so drunk she had gotten sick. I swear the dress was so tight that we had to help peel it off. She got dressed and flopped the dress on the counter and declared that she was not too fat for the dress that she was just constipated and she would go home and take something and the dress would fit her tomorrow. She left and I looked at one of my customers that was listening and watching the whole soap opera. "HA!!", she declared, "It will take more than X-Lax to get her fat butt into that dress. When she sobers up, she will wonder where that dress came from". Well I thought to myself, I hope she doesn't remember where she got it or who sold it to her.

YOUR HEADLIGHTS ARE ON!!

We have a lot of lunch hour business women that come in every week. We have three ladies that came in today and they were a hoot. They were all 50ish and fussing about how getting old is Hell! One of them is named Debbie. She was selecting items that are "younger than she needs" type clothes. You know sheer blouses and skin tight pants and skirts. She put on a blouse that was sheer and silky and came out of the dressing room to ask her friends what they thought. One of them was from Georgia and she offered up the first opinion. "Well sugar, if you are trying out for Debbie Does Dallas, it is perfect for you." Another of the ladies came running to see what a Debbie Does Dallas blouse looks like. She then declared, "OMG your headlights are on, quick cover up before that guy sees you". That guy was my husband. As usual he was sitting at the computer acting like he was very busy working. They finally bought a few things and left. The first thing my husband said, "What in the world did headlights have to do with buying a blouse?" I said, "Oh nothing much, just her boobies were standing at attention, that's all". Not another word. He just said, "Okeeee!."

NATIVE AMERICAN BOOBIES

𝓘t is now the middle of summer and business slows down some when the snowbirds leave to go back up north. Not much going on all morning. Around 11:00 two ladies came in and two more ladies came in directly behind them. They were all laughing and talking and looking over the clothes and shoes. I heard one of them tell the others, "You know I am Italian and I can wear just about any color known to mankind. I look good in any color." "OK", everyone agreed. That is nice. They continue on with their shopping. In a few minutes one of them said, "I am older and have no ass at all anymore, so I can wear almost anything tight fitting". That is nice they all agreed. By now they had all gathered up things to try on and a couple of them put on sun dresses and declared their boobs were to droopy and butts to fat to wear anything clingy. After feeling each other up and pushing each other's boobs up where they were supposed to be, they both agreed they needed new bras and spanx in order to wear light-weight silky sundresses. Well, last but not least, probably the oldest among them came out of the dressing room with a spaghetti strap silky dress. "Oh dear Lord, what a wonderful bra you have on. Your boobs look great", declared one lady. "What bra she said, I never wear a bra". "Not possible", the other ladies told her, "You have to be wearing a bra. Your boobs are perfect". She stood up tall and straight and declared, "My mother always told me that our boobs were naturally beautiful because we are Native American and Native American women have firm upright boobs." At that point she pulled her spaghetti straps down and showed all the women her Native American Boobs. They all declared they were amazing and she was glowing. Two of them paid for their items and left. I said well, "Look at them, they are not even waiting for you all". "Oh we don't know them, they were just in the last two stores we went to and we liked them so we just started talking to them when they came in here behind us." I was thinking when they all left. Just think that woman showed her Native American Boobies to total strangers. Miracles will never cease to happen in this place.

PARADISE

e were checking in clothing from our consignors, when a young lady and her mother came in to the shop. They were from the country of Texas. I completely blocked out and ignored anyone or anything else for the next hour, because I was in Heaven talking about Texas, the wonderful Austin Hill country, big hair, and cattle with big horns. The mother still lives in Texas and the daughter just moved to Sarasota with her husband. Her husband was born and raised in Sarasota. He believes Florida is the best state in the country. He and his best friend call Sarasota "Paradise". The daughter had left a wonderful job of six years with a Rodeo and Horse Association. She is very homesick for Texas. We visited and talked awhile and they left. Before leaving the daughter said she would be back next Saturday with her friend that has just moved here.

GOD FORSAKEN HELL HOLE

Well, a week had passed and here comes my little Texas Friend. She brought her friend, who had just moved here. We were introduced and I asked the fatal question, "Well, how do you like Florida?" She screeched it all out at once. "Oh My God, my husband told me we were going to retire to paradise. I told him he had moved me to nothing more than a God forsaken Hell Hole. I came from New York. The people up there are very polite compared to the mean, crazy people here. I have never seen so many idiots in my life. They are the rudest people in the world. My God, I never dreamed I would be living in a hell hole like this. I told him I'd give it one year and if I still hate it here, I am leaving with or without him. That's it! One Year". "Okee dokee", I said, "Do you have any energy left to look around and shop? I just put out shorts and blouses—long, long pause—. Then she started crying and said "I mean it. I hate it here". I put my arms around her and said, "I know you do, Honey. A lot of the people that are mean to you are probably Republicans". That broke the ice. My husband broke out the bottled water and we all toasted this "Hell Hole called Paradise".

TEXAS TORNADO

We left the house a little late this morning. We live no more than three minutes from the consignment shop. I told my husband to gun it! We were late and they would be waiting outside the door for us. He said, "We are so close, that by the time I gun it, we'll be there". We pulled in the parking lot and some nut drove up beside us like a bat out of hell. Pulled in and screeched on the brakes. First words out of my mouth, "Crap it is another large size woman craving a cupcake. Be careful getting out of the car, you may get trampled". I felt a little silly when I saw the car door open and my little petite friend, from the Pet grooming place, jumped out of her car and ran over to me. She is the only person I have ever met that is more hyper than me. She started rattling about, "What a jackass my husband is, and had I seen our mutual friend lately, and how is business, and she had three dogs to groom this morning, and one was a great Dane, and that was how she broke her back last year by lifting a big dog, and how her Dachshund bit her 18 year old Yorkie, and she grabbed him by the back of the neck and pulled up until his eyes nearly popped out. He will never bite her Yorkie again. Poor little Yorkie is blind and deaf and I have to hurry because I am going to the big mall in Tampa this afternoon. See you later, Bye!" My husband heard it all and made the comment, "That lady talks faster than a Texas Tornado. One of these days she is going to get wound up and it will take a cattle prod to shut her up".

Texas Tornado

LITTLE BANTY ROOSTER

This is Saturday morning and we have been very busy. The dressing rooms needed revolving doors.

There were ladies waiting their turn to try on clothes. The front door opens and it is an elderly couple.

Cutest little couple ever. He stands inside holding the door open for her. As she enters the shop, he declares very loudly, "You have fifteen minutes". She looks up at him, points her finger very firmly and yells, "Sit". He immediately dropped into one of the 'husband' chairs by the front door. Just like a puppy! He was a good boy for the next hour and a half. My husband finally felt sorry for him and took him a newspaper and a bottled water. They talked awhile about how women really do run this world, Lots of their conversation was in whispers. Probably didn't want to ruffle the little banty rooster's feathers. She came out of the dressing room, put the things she wanted on the counter. She then walked up front and without a word, he got up and walked to the register and paid for her purchases. I put everything in a bag and she directed me to hand the bag to her husband. They walked out the front door. Total silence—-—A young man standing there while his wife was looking at clothes, looked at my husband and asked, "Is that what happens when you get old?" All my husband said was, "Yep! And there is nothing you can do to stop it. Your dignity is the first thing to go".

SHUT THE DAMN DOOR.

We have had our week-end, Sunday and Monday and are ready to start the week on Tuesday morning.

We drive up to the shop and my husband gets out of the car first. He always goes in ahead of me, so he can turn off the security alarm. Today was no different. He unlocked the front door and heads for the alarm. I waited in the car for him to wave for me to come in. This is always our routine. The alarm will not shut off if the door is not closed. Here he is standing at the alarm, ready to disarm it and out of nowhere; this little old lady appeared and holds the door open. My husband yells, "Shut the door, please, I need to turn off the alarm". She just stood there holding the door open. He yelled again, "Please close the door". I saw what was happening and yelled out of the car window, "Shut the door!" She never moved, just stood there holding the door wide open. I got out of the car screaming, "Shut the door, the alarm is about to go off". She didn't move. After three times screaming "shut the door", I finally got so frustrated, I yelled "Shut the damn door!" About that time the siren started blasting. I pushed her inside, shut the door and My husband turned off the alarm. I said the phone is about to ring and it will be the security company. Sure enough the phone rang. It was security and they immediately asked me for the security code. I just stood there and babbled out, "This is the first time in a year that this sucker has gone off". He said, "I'm sorry, Mam, but

I have to have the code now or I will have to dispatch the police". "OMG, do you know anything about the police in this area. They will shoot me just because I am from Texas and talk funny!". He said, "Mam, give me the code right now!". I said, "OK, OK, is it "sweatin' bullets". "No Mam", "OK, just kidding!, is it "Boo?"—no, Dudley?"—no."" Mam, just give me the code. Right now!". I yelled, "I can't remember the code" and started blubbering like a baby and I told him, "If you call the cops, what happens is your fault". "Alright, Mam, just calm down and tell me what code word you would use if you were making up a new one now" I blurted out, "Grits". He said, "That is it, why didn't you tell me that to begin with? Have a good day, Mam". The lady that caused this entire ruckus, looked around a few minutes and then said, "I set my friends alarm off a few weeks ago where I was dog sitting. I didn't have the code word and they called the police. It wasn't so bad! Took a while to get it all straightened out though". She left. . . I wanted to follow her down the sidewalk and tackle her and beat the words "I am sorry" out of her. My husband didn't think that would be a good idea.

ARE MY KNEES TOO FAT?

This is the day of many different awkward moments. Mid-morning, a rather plump lady came out of the dressing room. As usual, my husband was sitting at his desk doing his computer work. The lady was trying on a very short skirt. She looked at my husband and asked, "Is this skirt too short for my fat knees?" He looked up and over at her knees. I could tell he was struggling for the right answer. Total silence—finally he speaks, "I think it is the skirt, not your knees. You might try a longer length over your knees. I bet you would like it better". OMG, you would have thought he was a world famous clothing expert. She ran back into the dressing room and put on a longer dress. Then she came out for his approval. Her question was, "Well, what about this length, Pops?" His reply to her, "Now you're talking! That's the perfect length". She was happy with his help. He was very happy with his answer. I was very happy we got through another "Am I too fat crisis".

POLO RACE

$\mathcal{B}$oy, what a busy day. People coming in from everywhere. One right after another.

Mid-morning, a skinny little lady came in like gang busters. She flung the front door open and headed for the rack where the T-shirts and Polo shirts were hanging. She flew around the rack with me running right behind her. At the end of the rack, she rounded the corner and all of a sudden she slammed on her brakes at the front checkout counter. Ira watched as I rounded the corner at full speed and almost rear ended her.

She said, "Your prices are too high!" OMG, I was winded from the foot race I just had with her. I looked at her very sternly and asked, "And how, pray tell, could you even see my pricing at the breakneck speed you were going?" She said, "Your store looks too nice to carry a $2.00 Polo shirt. I have been out of work for two years. I just got a job and I have to wear Polo shirts. All I have is $2.00". "Well, why didn't you just tell me that when you came in"?

"It would have saved that big "polo" race thru the building. Follow me". I pulled three shirts off the rack and snapped the tags off. Put the shirts in a bag and handed it to her. She said, "I can't pay for them". I told her, "Not to worry, the old guy at the checkout counter would take care of the bill". She thanked me and left the building. Everyone in the shop looked relieved that things had quieted down and everyone was happy. Ira took care of the accounting part of the transaction. He said, "That was a very kind thing for you to do". I said, "Well, thank ya! See, sometimes I can be nice if I want to be".

I just figured the lady was another victim of the Bank of America or Countrywide fiasco like we were. You know the part where they say to you after you buy the house you can't really afford. "Oh yes, now you can take out a line of credit for a God awful endless amount and we have you by the 'ying yang', till death do us part. End of story". Ira said, "Yeah, till death almost did its part. Liked to killed both of us, didn't it?"

HAIR OF MANY COLORS

We had a young lady and her Mom come in today. The young lady was about 18-19 years old and was cute in a weird sort of way. Her hair was four shades of pastel colors. Front was hot pink, sides lime green and the back was lemon yellow and tangerine orange. Cute, cute face and hair cut but hmmmm—the colors were a little exotic.

Her Mom was very pretty and dressed very conservative. She was an older Mom and spoke with a German accent. The daughter was very rude and mean to her. Every time her Mom tried to show her a dress, she snapped, "Stop trying to get me to buy something you like. I hate the clothes you pick out". The poor Mom acted like she was afraid of the girl. I finally stepped in and offered my professional expertise. I wanted to bitch slap her into the next century, but I controlled myself. I said, "Tell me, my dear, what is it you are looking for? What colors do you like?" As if I didn't already know by the color of her hair. "It's not really what I like, but what I need. I am going to apply for a sales job at the Lilly Pulitzer store in Tampa and I dyed my hair to match the colors Lilly uses in her clothing line. I need Lilly clothes to match my hair". I thought to myself, OMG this girl is either very creative or a total dumb butt. Think I know which one it is.

I said, "Okay, but first I am going to give you a little advise. Trust me, you need to get rid of the pastel hair colors. The Lilly people will not be impressed. They probably will not even give you an interview. Just my opinion". She flipped around to her Mom and asked, "Did you tell her to say that?" Her Mom said, "No, why should I tell her to say that, I don't even know this lady". The daughter stomped out the front door. Her Mom thanked me and left the shop. Ira said, "Don't you think that went well?" "No, not really because she did not stick around for my speech on how she should treat her Mother better!"

HOT TEXAS BOYFRIEND

$\mathcal{T}$oday is turning out to be "Girls Day Out". We have lots of tourists coming into the shop. Four older ladies came in and man, were they wound up. They grew up together and went to school together. After high school they all went their separate ways. They told stories about how they married, divorced and one was a widow. They all get together once a year. They had some wild and woolly stories.

Naturally they mentioned that I talked funny. They asked where I grew up. "The country of Texas" was my loud answer. Now we are off and running. We covered everything from hot biscuits and gravy, chicken fried steak to oil wells, boots and big hair. We moved on to the blankets of bluebonnets all along the highways in the spring time. Ahhhha. Not one mention of Bush, Jr. We went onto sing the praises of former governor Ann Richards. Everything was going along "honkey, dorey" and the tall, slender brunette made the statement that, "I found the men from Texas to be extremely sexy, with their tight jeans and cowboy boots. Didn't you?"

OMG, I forgot where I was. I said, "Oh yes!!" She was telling us about a really "tall drink of water" or maybe it was a "tall drink of whiskey". He looked like the Marlborough Man. "Oh my Lordy, he was a dream. I went out with him for over a year and then his wife put a stop to it.

Wheeew, he was one hot Texas Cowboy". My response, "Oh Honey, I can beat that one. When I was 32 years old, I had the biggest flaming hottest affair known to mankind. He was the—". About that time, Ira shot up out of his chair and stood straight up behind his desk. He looked over his glasses like, "Don't even go there". I had forgotten he was back there. Didn't forget it for long because his roller chair banged against the wall. I snapped back to reality and said, "Oh that story is for another day. One of the ladies grinned and asked, "Is that your husband?" "Yep!" Then I walked them to the front of the store. When they were leaving, one of them said, "The biggest, hottest, flaming affair known to mankind. Wow, that must have been some man. I can just imagine the rest of the story". I said, "No you can't. It was more hotness than you could ever imagine". They all looked puzzled. "Did you make that up or is it true". "It is true". "Well, how did it end?" "He died". "How?" "Heart attack". Total silence—"Well, see you next year, we will be back. We will definitely come back to your shop. This was really interesting and lots of fun".

THE STUPID ASS COMPUTER

The month of July is usually a little slower for the business. We have noticed it is quiet in the mornings and people start coming in after lunch. We put the time to good use. The "Stupid Ass" computer, (my nickname for it) decided to freeze up. I kept after Ira for the next hour, until he froze up. I whined and whined for him to call the repair guy to fix the computer. He insisted he could fix it.

I kept whining that the customer's would be coming in the door any minute. "Hurry! Hurry! Hurry!" I said, "You know I hate it when we look stupid to people. That was the final blow for him. He shoved the keyboard back so hard it crunched against his tax papers and that in turn flipped his fresh cup of coffee. It was like a Texas flash flood.—across his desk and into his drawers. No, not his desk drawers—I mean his under drawers. He immediately jumped to his feet and yelled, "Hell, now you have done it!" I knew this was a Lucy and Ricky moment because he never used bad words.

I grabbed a roll of paper towels and tossed it to him as I raced for the front door. I yelled, "I am going home to get you dry unders. I will be right back". Half hour later, I was back with dry clothes. He was sitting in his desk chair and not moving. I said, "Has anyone been in?" He said, "Yes, but I think she thought I was rude, because I never got up out my chair". He changed his clothes and went back to wasting the next two hours trying to fix the "stupid ass" computer. I was using the little hand calculator to figure out the purchases.

He finally gave in and called the computer repair shop and the guy came down and punched two buttons and charged $80.00. He left and we were up and running. We gave each other those little "go to smiles" and got back to work.

FIRST YEAR ANIVERSARY

*W*hen we pulled up in front of the building this morning, it came to us that we have made it through our first year. This first year flew away faster than our family and friends when we lost our money.

We are very aware of how many people have been crushed harder than we were by this recession.

Families with small children were hit the hardest because so many of them lost jobs.

The material things we lost mean nothing now. We realize those things were not who we are. We need very little to be happy. We had to swallow our pride, suck it up and start over again. We just didn't think we would be doing it at our age.

Note:

The names in these stories were either changed or omitted to protect the innocent, obnoxious and the crazy people who came in to our shop.

ABOUT THE AUTHOR

$\mathcal{P}$eggy Ann was born in Kentucky and raised in Texas. She was operating her own business before the term "woman owned business" was invented. She has owned several businesses. The little Consignment Shop she now owns is one of her favorites. She is a pioneer for other women that want to own their own business.

Peggy Ann never forgets her humble beginnings in life. She grew up in Abilene, Texas and ended up in Arlington, Texas running a large Advertising Specialty Company. She attributes her "Drama Queen" personality to her Texas upbringing and her mother's side of the family. She had a beautiful blonde mother and a wonderful Christian Grandmother. Spilled milk could create a very dramatic crisis for the women in the family. Her husband, Ira, has learned after 25 years together to deal with her. He says he deals with her drama one of two ways. No time for that or just go ahead and do your thing and whine and get it over with. Ira see's the "Drama Queen Personality" as being very entertaining and creative. It seems to be good for both of them. They have a very successful marriage and another successful business venture together.

Peggy Ann is currently living in Sarasota, Florida. She and her husband work together to keep Peggy Ann's Chic Boutique successful and operating smoothly. They make a great team. She is the hyper member of the team, while Ira is the calm member of the team.

In all the years Peggy Ann and Ira have been together, they have been rich and they have been poor. Peggy Ann never hesitates when asked which is better. Her reply is always loud and clear. "Don't expect me to give you that crap, you can be happy, no matter how much or how little money you have. I grew up dirt poor and hated it. Being rich is far better. Just not Republican Rich".